Hocus Pocus!

Mikki had replaced the stopper in the vial and started to walk inside when she noticed a strange feeling at the top of her head. It was kind of a warm tingling, a bit like an electric shock, but not painful. In fact, it was rather pleasant. The tingling moved down her head to her neck and then spread to her shoulders, her arms, her fingertips. By the time she reached the front porch her whole body was throbbing with the strange tingling.

It's working, Mikki realized with a mixture of disbelief and excitement. *The spell is working!*

Phantom Valley™

The Spell

Lynn Beach

A MINSTREL® BOOK

PUBLISHED BY POCKET BOOKS

New York   London   Toronto   Sydney   Tokyo   Singapore

This book is a work of fiction. Names, characters, places, and incidents are either the product of the author's imagination or are used fictitiously. Any resemblance to actual events or locales or persons, living or dead, is entirely coincidental.

A MINSTREL PAPERBACK *ORIGINAL*

 A Minstrel Book published by
POCKET BOOKS, a division of Simon & Schuster Inc.
1230 Avenue of the Americas, New York, NY 10020

ISBN: 0-671-75923-X

First Minstrel Books printing June 1992

10 9 8 7 6 5 4 3 2 1

A MINSTREL BOOK and colophon are registered trademarks
of Simon & Schuster Inc.

Printed in the U.S.A.

To RBI and Hatshe

The Spell

CHAPTER 1

MIKKI Merrill stepped out of the taxi and studied the huge, old-fashioned wooden building. Her stomach fluttered nervously as she read the gold letters on the black sign attached to the roof of the rambling porch: CHILLEEN ACADEMY.

I'm back, she thought. *I wonder what will happen this year.* Mikki waved as the taxi driver took off down the long, unpaved driveway to the Silverbell Road. She took a deep breath of the warm western air. Then she just stood for a moment, taking in the large front lawn and beautiful pine forest that backed the building. During the school year the grounds would be filled with boys and girls, shouting, laughing, playing sports, or doing work-study jobs. But that day the grounds were empty. Even the teachers' parking lot to one side of the building had very few cars in it. The loudest sound was the wind.

The day for student arrivals was the next one, but

Mikki had to come early because both her parents left on a business trip. *Maybe I'm the first person here,* she thought. She felt a little shiver as she remembered all the stories she'd heard about Phantom Valley when she first arrived the year before—stories about how the woods around the school, and even the boarding school itself, were haunted.

Stop it, Mikki, she told herself. *You were here a whole year, and nothing strange happened even once.*

She opened the heavy wooden front door, then picked up her bags and stepped into the entrance hall. Her footsteps echoed noisily in the huge old mansion. She could hear the creaking of the wooden floor.

On her left was the dayroom, with its leather and wood furniture and framed western prints. It was completely empty. Mikki started to walk through the room to her dormitory wing, then stopped and sank into one of the cowhide chairs. There was no reason to hurry. Jenny wouldn't be waiting for her this year. Mikki wasn't quite ready to face an empty dorm room or an unknown roommate.

Until the previous week, Mikki had been excited about returning to school. She had been planning to room with her best friend, Jenny Hollis. Then Jenny had called with the bad news—her father had been transferred to Florida, and Jenny would be going to school there.

It's not fair, Mikki thought. But there wasn't anything she could do about it. She had made several friends last year, but there was no one she cared about as much as Jenny. *I'm all alone now,* thought Mikki, biting her lip nervously. She had wondered whether she'd be given a single room. Then her final room assignment had arrived—she'd be in her old room again. That meant a new roommate.

Taking a deep breath, Mikki picked up her bags and started climbing the stairs to her floor. She could hear the happy, excited voices of a few other Chilleen students. She could also hear Mrs. Danita, the headmistress, talking with a student down the hall. At least, Mikki thought, she wasn't the only one there.

By the time she got to her old familiar room, she was beginning to be excited. Sure, she'd miss Jenny, but there were plenty of things she liked about Chilleen and Phantom Valley. She'd be able to hike, and swim, and, most important of all, start her ballet classes again. The Chilleen teacher, Mrs. Braine, was the best dance instructor Mikki had ever had. Mikki hoped Mrs. Braine would give her the solo in the first dance recital. The first recital was just six weeks after the year started.

Still thinking about the recital, Mikki entered the old-fashioned room with its dark-wood trim and sloping ceilings. She started to put her suitcase on her bed, the one nearest the window. Then she saw that someone had already taken that side of the room. There was a teddy bear on her bed.

So my new roommate's here already, she thought, and the nervous flutterings started again in her stomach. *She's probably someone new,* Mikki decided. Nearly all the students from last year had picked their roommates before summer vacation.

Mikki took her things to the other side of the room and

started to unpack. Soon she heard the door opening. She was excited to see who her new roommate would be.

One look at the blond girl in the doorway and Mikki felt her stomach drop. Standing there was the last person she wanted to see, let alone have as a roommate. It was Diane Mason.

CHAPTER 2

"**D**IANE!" said Mikki. She was so surprised and upset she couldn't think of anything else to say.

"Mikki." Diane seemed equally surprised—and upset.

"Is—is this your room?" Mikki asked. She already knew the answer but was hoping Diane would say no.

"Of course it is," said Diane. "Where's Jenny?"

"She moved to Florida—she's not coming back this year," Mikki said.

Diane stood awkwardly in the door. Mikki just stared at her, not knowing what else to do.

"This should be some year," Mikki muttered under her breath.

"Well, I never wanted to room with you, either!" Diane said angrily.

"If Jenny had come back to school like she was supposed to, none of this would have happened," Mikki said. "I bet Mrs. Danita still thinks we're friends and that's why she put us together."

"Well, we're not—not anymore," answered Diane. She crossed her arms in front of her chest.

"Fine with me," Mikki said coldly and turned back to her suitcase. She began to unwrap her collection of small ballerina figures and arrange them on her dresser. She could feel Diane's hot stare.

"Are you really going to put those things out?" asked Diane in a shrill voice. "Don't you think they're little-girlish?"

"I like them, and they're staying!" Mikki answered, louder than she'd meant to.

"Well, okay," said Diane, making it obvious that she didn't like them.

Mikki wished more than anything that Jenny were here. Jenny liked Mikki's little dancers and loved ballet almost as much as Mikki.

"Jenny told me you were supposed to be in a single room this year," said Mikki.

"We can both see that I'm not," Diane answered, staring down at the floor.

"Look, Diane, this certainly wasn't my idea, but if we've got to room together, we might as well make the best of it," Mikki said, her voice shaking.

A long heavy silence followed.

"Sure, whatever," Diane finally said. "I've got to get out of here. I'm going horseback riding." She pulled a denim jacket out of the closet, then left the room as if she couldn't wait to get out.

Feeling more miserable than ever, Mikki threw herself facedown on her bed. How could she survive the year living with horrible Diane? Tears welled up in her eyes.

6

Suddenly a familiar voice called from the door. "Knock, knock!"

Mikki rolled over and sat up to see Ellen Bright and her older brother Mark standing just inside the room. Their round faces were both smiling broadly, and Mikki couldn't help grinning in return. "Ellen!" she said. "Mark! I'm so happy to see you!"

"You, too!" said Ellen.

"We didn't think you'd be here today," Mark said.

"My parents both had to leave town on a business trip," answered Mikki. "To tell you the truth, I was afraid I might be the only person here."

"Don't worry," said Mark. "A lot of the teachers are already here, and some of the kids. I see your roommate has arrived."

"Where *is* Jenny?" said Ellen.

"Jenny won't be here this year," said Mikki, feeling down again. "Her parents moved, and they thought Chilleen was too far away."

"Too bad," said Ellen. "Then who's your roommate?"

"You won't believe this," said Mikki. "Diane Mason."

"You're kidding!" said Ellen. "But you two don't get along at all."

"I know," said Mikki glumly.

"I never understood what happened," said Mark. "Last year you and Diane and Jenny were all really good friends. Some of the guys called you the Three Musketeers. Then all of a sudden, at the end of the year, you and Diane were hardly speaking. What's the story?"

"I wish I knew," Mikki answered. "It started when we had to pick roommates for this year. Jenny and Diane had

7

roomed together last year. Well, Jenny told me that Diane really wanted a single room. So Jenny and I asked to live together."

"What happened then?" asked Mark.

"I don't know," Mikki continued. "For no reason, Diane stopped talking to the two of us. She acted all cold and snooty. Then during the last week of school she yelled at me in the dayroom and embarrassed me in front of all the kids. She criticized me and called me immature and a nerd. I was so angry."

"Maybe Mrs. Danita will let you switch," suggested Ellen.

"I don't think so," Mikki said. "You know her policy of no switching."

"Don't worry so much," said Mark. "You and Diane were good friends once. Maybe you can work things out."

Mikki wanted with all her heart to believe Mark, but deep down she knew it wouldn't happen. Diane Mason still hated her. She lay back down on her bed and declared, "This whole year is going to be a disaster, I just know it."

By the second week of school Mikki still found life with Diane unbearable. Diane hadn't done anything really mean to Mikki, but the girls hardly spoke, except when it was absolutely necessary, and Diane was cold and self-absorbed. She spent what seemed like hours brushing, combing, and conditioning her long, thick, blond hair and ignoring Mikki. Mikki had been so excited when she found out she was one of the finalists for the dance solo in the recital, but she didn't even think of telling Diane. She knew Diane wouldn't care.

The second week of school was when the students began their required work-study programs. Each student was assigned to a different job. Most kids worked at the school, but a few got to work in the nearby town of Silverbell. When Mikki saw her work-study posted on the bulletin board, she broke out in a big smile. It was just what she wanted.

She rushed to her room after classes that day to change for her job. Unfortunately, Diane was already there, sitting on her bed and doing her math.

Mikki changed into a clean T-shirt and then began combing her hair, trying to make it lie all in one direction. But her mousy-brown hair was frizzier than ever and stood out all over her head. She became aware that Diane was watching her and felt embarrassed.

"Where are you going?" Diane asked curiously.

"My new work-study," said Mikki.

"Oh, really?" said Diane. "What do you have? I'm working in the school office." She said it as if it were the most important job at Chilleen.

"I'm working in Silverbell," said Mikki.

"For real?" said Diane, sounding impressed in spite of herself. "What are you doing there?"

"It's a great job," said Mikki, unable to hide her enthusiasm. "I'm going to be reading to an old lady with bad eyesight."

"You're going to *what?*" said Diane, as if Mikki had told her she was going to be breeding cockroaches.

"Her name's Mrs. Hazel Wembley, and she lives in a trailer park on the outskirts of town," Mikki went on. "I'm looking forward to it. I like old people. It will be like visiting my grandmother."

"Sounds thrilling," said Diane, her tone of voice showing she thought it was anything but thrilling.

Mikki didn't even bother to answer. She put her comb away and ran her fingers through her hair one last time. "See you later," she said coldly. She tied her denim jacket around her shoulders, then ran out of the room and down to the bus stop. She didn't want to be late meeting the other kids who also were going into Silverbell for their first work-study session. It was a perfect late-summer day, and the bright sky and fresh mountain air made her forget Diane for a moment.

The Silverbell bus was on time. Besides the group from Chilleen, there were only a few other people on the bus, mostly ranch hands and a few Native Americans from the nearby reservation. As the bus drove through the thick pine forest, she could see through the back window, the foot hills, where Shadow Village, a crumbling Native American settlement, was. Mikki had never believed any of the spooky stories about it. To her Phantom Valley was the most beautiful place in the world, even if other people said strange things sometimes happened there.

The bus turned from the red-dirt road onto the paved highway to Silverbell, and twenty-five minutes later it pulled up at the bus station across from the town plaza. The group from Chilleen got out and started walking to the far side of town.

Mikki went to the ticket window to ask directions to Mrs. Wembley's.

"You want to go to Merney Park?" said the ticket clerk in obvious disbelief. "Are you sure?"

"Why not?" asked Mikki, startled.

"It's really run-down," the woman said. "And it's not in a very nice part of town."

"I have an appointment there," Mikki insisted. "With someone who lives in the trailer park."

"It's hard to believe anyone actually lives there," muttered the ticket lady. She drew Mikki a little map, and Mikki followed it, taking Main Street to a dirt road that led to the edge of some woods. At first she thought she had followed the directions wrong, but then she saw a sign: "Merney Park, trailer space by the week or month."

She understood now what the woman in the bus station had meant. The trailer park *was* run-down. It seemed to be empty. The grounds were choked with thick weeds. Overgrown trees cast unfriendly shadows. Most of the once-silver trailers in the park were rusted now. A couple seemed to have people living in them, judging by the laundry drying outside.

One of the trailers near the front had a sign saying OFFICE. Right below the sign was a hand-lettered message on cardboard saying, BACK IN FIVE MINUTES. It looked as if it had been there for five years, not five minutes.

Feeling nervous, Mikki decided to try to find Mrs. Wembley's trailer, H-5, herself. She walked among the trailers, but there didn't seem to be any organization to the numbering of the trailers. Numbers A-1 and L-15 sat side by side, and several trailers didn't have any numbers. As Mikki wandered around, the only other person she saw was a small boy playing with a plastic water gun. Perhaps she shouldn't have come alone.

She did finally find H-5, the best looking of all the trailers. Still, it was dented and old. Trying not to feel nervous, Mikki approached the front door and knocked. There was no answer, so she knocked again, louder.

"That's funny," she said aloud. She knew she had come on the right day, Tuesday afternoon. Once again she knocked, and again there was no answer. By now Mikki had become aware of a strange odor coming from inside the trailer. An odor of decay or of something rotting.

More nervous than ever, she knocked again, as hard as she could. Mrs. Wembley was old and might be a little hard of hearing, but she knew Mikki was coming. Then Mikki noticed that her last knocking had opened the door partway.

She slowly pushed it open. It was dark inside the trailer, and crowded, and at first Mikki couldn't make out anything. Then she caught a small movement. Sitting in an antique rocking chair was a small, stooped figure who must be Mrs. Wembley. Tall black candles were burning on tables at either side of the chair. The old woman was hunched over and seemed to be polishing something. She didn't seem to know that Mikki was there. Mikki opened her mouth to speak, then stopped, shocked, when she saw what the old woman was polishing.

It was round and white with dark eye sockets and a

dead, toothy grin. Mikki realized with horror that the old woman was polishing a human skull!

Mikki's heart was beating so hard she could hardly breathe. She couldn't take her eyes off the old woman, who just kept polishing the skull with a red velvet cloth. Suddenly something jumped out of one of the skull's gaping eyeholes and ran onto the old woman's shoulder!

CHAPTER 3

IKKI shrieked and jumped back to the doorway. The old woman raised her head and gave Mikki a warm smile. "Why, hello," she said. "You must be the girl from Chilleen."

Mikki was too startled to answer. As she watched, the old woman casually reached up to her shoulder. The thing that had jumped out of the skull was still sitting there. Now Mikki realized it was a tiny white mouse.

"I'm—I'm Mikki Merrill," Mikki said breathlessly.

"I'm Mrs. Wembley," said the old woman. She picked up the mouse. "And this is my little pet," she added. She placed the mouse back inside the skull, through an eyehole, then put the skull on one of the tables.

"I'm so glad to meet you, dear," Mrs. Wembley said. She slowly stood up, and Mikki could see that she was so stooped and feeble that she couldn't stand up straight. She was wearing bright yellow stretch pants, a yellow cotton tank top, and black Converse hightops. She had on a pair of thick glasses, and she was squinting through them as if she couldn't see clearly.

"I kept knocking and knocking," Mikki said then.

"I'm terribly sorry," said Mrs. Wembley. "I'm a little hard of hearing. Well, let me just turn down the stove and we'll talk." She hobbled over to the kitchen area and turned a knob on the stove. Mikki realized the strange odor she'd smelled was coming from a huge cast-iron pot on one of the burners.

"Whew!" said Mrs. Wembley. "It smells terrible, doesn't it?"

"Maybe we should open a window," Mikki suggested.

"Good idea," said Mrs. Wembley. "Go ahead while I put this pot in the sink."

Mikki opened a front window. "What were you cooking?" she asked.

"Why, it's a love potion," said Mrs. Wembley airily.

"A love—" said Mikki, and then she stopped, laughing. *What a great sense of humor,* she thought. Mrs. Wembley was older than Mikki's grandmother, but she dressed more like a teenager. Mikki wondered what it was going to be like working for her.

"I'll be with you in just a moment," the old woman said. "I only— Oh, drat!"

"What's wrong?" Mikki ran into the kitchen area just in time to see some of the strange-smelling contents splash onto the floor as Mrs. Wembley lifted the heavy pot. "Let me do that," said Mikki, grabbing a pot holder and taking over. "Wow, this is heavy."

"Yes," said Mrs. Wembley sadly. "Sometimes I forget I'm not as strong as I used to be."

As Mikki put the pot into the sink, she wondered how long Mrs. Wembley had been living alone. She'd never met anyone so old before. *OWWR!* Mikki jumped, startled, as a brown cat suddenly leapt out of a cabinet and onto the counter.

"So there you are, you naughty girl!" said Mrs. Wembley. "This is Ha-Chee," she told Mikki. "She's always hiding from me, aren't you, Hach?"

OWWR, said Ha-Chee again, settling down to wash her paws. Mikki couldn't take her eyes off her. Ha-Chee was the strangest-looking cat she'd ever seen, long and skinny with ears nearly as big as a fox's and a long, pointed tail.

"What kind of cat is that?" Mikki asked.

"She's a short-haired imp," said Mrs. Wembley.

"A what?" said Mikki. "I never heard of that kind of cat."

"Not many have," said the old woman. She kissed the little cat on the head, then picked up a mop that had been lying in the corner and, squinting, began to work on the small puddle that had poured out of the pot.

Mrs. Wembley's eyesight was so bad that she only smeared the puddle around. "Let me do that for you," Mikki said. "I don't mind."

"If you insist," said Mrs. Wembley, and she sat shakily in an antique chair against one wall. From the way she sat, Mikki could tell that she was more tired and feeble than she let on.

"Do you like R.E.M.?" Mrs. Wembley asked.

"What?" said Mikki. "You mean the music group?"

"Of course the music group," said Mrs. Wembley. "I

just got a new CD, and if you don't mind, I'll put it on while you finish cleaning up."

"I'd love it!" Mikki said. She listened to the CD, cleaning in rhythm to the music, until there was no trace of the foul green liquid or its smell. As she worked, she took a closer look around the trailer. Every inch was crammed with ancient furniture and knickknacks.

She knew her mom would love to see them. Her mother was an antique dealer, and Mikki recognized most of the furniture as genuine antiques. She was sure that some of the things were at least two hundred years old, which seemed very odd for trailer furniture. Probably, she decided, Mrs. Wembley had fallen on hard times and had moved from a huge old house.

"A penny for your thoughts, dear," said Mrs. Wembley.

"They aren't worth that much," said Mikki, suddenly embarrassed. "I was just thinking how beautiful your antique furniture is."

"Why, thank you," said Mrs. Wembley. "It's all so old now, like me. But when these things were new, they were beautiful!"

Mikki realized that if Mrs. Wembley had bought the furniture new, none of it could be antique. She guessed she didn't know how to spot antiques as well as she'd thought.

The CD had finished playing, and Mrs. Wembley sighed. "I know I've already taken up a great deal of your time today," she said. "But my eyes are too weak to read. And I do love stories. Would you mind just starting this new book I got from the bookmobile yesterday?"

'I'd be happy to," said Mikki. She settled beside the old woman on the couch and took the book. It was titled

Vampire Loves, and Mikki recognized it as a best-seller horror-romance. She almost laughed out loud. Rock 'n' roll and vampires! This job was going to be fun!

On the bus home from Silverbell, Mikki couldn't get the strange, charming old woman out of her mind. Everything about Mrs. Wembley was so unusual. She couldn't wait to tell Ellen and Mark about her. They'd never believe the old woman kept a mouse inside a skull and made love potions on her stove, or that she dressed in stretch pants and listened to rock music. Mikki couldn't believe how lucky she was.

She stepped off the bus and ran up the long driveway to the main academy building. She just had time to get upstairs and change for dinner. Whistling a tune from the R.E.M. CD, she walked quickly up the stairs to her dorm room. She pushed open the door and stopped when she heard Diane's voice.

"It's Mikki!" Diane was saying. She was sitting on her bed, her back to the door, the phone to her ear. "Mikki Merrill!" she continued, not aware of Mikki standing at the door. "That's right, the one who doesn't care about anything but ballet. Well, I have to room with her, do you believe it? I tell you, this is going to be the worst year of my life."

Mikki just stood in the door, her face burning from embarrassment and anger. All her good feelings from the afternoon were gone.

That night as Mikki studied she tried to ignore Diane. But as she worked on her homework, she couldn't help but be aware of her roommate, who was sitting on her bed with a towel around her head, giving her long hair a hot-oil treatment.

Mikki decided it might be easier to study in the day-room. She shut her book and was about to leave the room when there was a knock at the door. She cheered up at the sight of Ellen's round, smiling face. "Hi, Mikki," said Ellen. "Hi, Diane."

"Oh, hello, Ellen," Diane said as if she were doing her a favor by speaking.

"I need some help with the geography questions," Ellen announced. "And also I wanted to find out how your first day of work-study went."

"It was great!" Mikki said as she remembered the wonderful time she had had with Mrs. Wembley that afternoon. "You wouldn't believe what Mrs. Wembley is like."

"How old is she?" asked Ellen, sitting next to Mikki on her bed.

"In her eighties, I think," Mikki answered. "But you'd never know it from the way she acts. She wears stretch pants and likes to listen to rock CDs, and—"

"What a weirdo!" Diane interrupted from across the room.

"No one asked you," said Mikki, stung.

"I'm going down to Anita's room," said Diane. "Maybe I can find someone who has something *interesting* to talk about." She knotted the towel tighter around her head and swept out of the room.

"I don't believe her!" said Ellen.

"I do, unfortunately," said Mikki.

"Well, just forget about her," said Ellen. "Everyone knows she's a conceited jerk."

"It's more than that," said Mikki. "She treats me like I'm a—a baby or something. She criticizes everything I say or do."

"If you ask me," said Ellen, "she's jealous of you."

"Jealous? Diane? Of *me?*"

"Sure," said Ellen. "You're the best dancer in the whole school, you make good grades—"

"But Diane's really popular," Mikki protested. "And beautiful. I've always wanted to look like her, with long blond hair."

"*She* doesn't know that," said Ellen. "Besides, remember that Diane and Jenny were close friends since elementary school. She probably thinks *you* don't like *her*. And then Jenny chose to room with you, not her."

Mikki didn't answer for a moment. Could it be true? Should she try to be nicer to Diane? They had been friends before. Maybe they could be again.

Feeling a little better, Mikki finished telling Ellen what had happened with Mrs. Wembley. Ellen was so fascinated that she forgot all about her geography homework. By the time she left, it was late. Mikki reopened her English textbook but couldn't make herself concentrate. All she could think of was Diane and what Ellen had said.

Mikki finally shut her English book, giving up on homework for the night. Diane still hadn't returned from Anita's room. Mikki went to her desk and searched around in the top drawer. In the back among her scissors and papers was a small, leather-bound green book. It was her diary. She'd been keeping a diary ever since she was a small girl, and she found that writing about things helped her deal with her problems.

As she wrote about what had happened with Mrs. Wembley and her feelings about Diane, she lost track of time. When she finished, she replaced the diary in the drawer, feeling much better. *Somehow*, she thought, *I'm going to learn to get along with Diane.*

For the next few days Mikki and Diane hardly spoke to each other, which suited Mikki just fine. She was so busy she barely had time to think about her roommate, anyway. In addition to her schoolwork, every day she had to work on her solo for the midterm dance recital. Then, too, she met with Mrs. Wembley two times a week after school.

The more she saw of the old woman, the more she liked her. Every time Mikki visited, Mrs. Wembley was wearing a different and more outrageous outfit. One day it was bicycle pants with a bright fuchsia sweatshirt. Another time it was a long green gown with stars and planets embroidered all over it. "You like it?" Mrs. Wembley asked, modeling the gown for Mikki. "I made it myself many years ago, when my eyesight was still sharp."

One day when Mikki had finished reading Mrs. Wembley's library book, she offered to read to the old woman from one of the books on her shelves. "Those?" said Mrs. Wembley with a giggle. "I doubt very much that you *could* read them."

"What do you mean?" said Mikki. She got up and began to examine the nearest row of books on the long bookcase that covered one wall of the trailer from floor to ceiling. She looked closely at the titles, and then saw what the old woman meant. Nearly every book was written in a foreign language. Some of the languages were common ones that Mikki could recognize, like French and Spanish. But many of the books seemed to be written in strange alphabets, with odd-looking squiggles instead of regular letters.

"How many languages do you know?" Mikki asked, astonished.

"I'm not sure," said Mrs. Wembley. "Several. I've had a long time to learn them."

Mikki shook her head in amazement. She had never, in her whole life, known anyone as interesting as Mrs. Wembley. "What are the books about?" Mikki asked.

"Oh, they're on every subject imaginable," said the old woman. "There are cookbooks, and travel books, and poetry books. There are books on history, on psychology, on chiromancy. . . ."

"On what?" said Mikki, intrigued.

"That's the scientific term for palm reading," said Mrs. Wembley. "It used to be something of a hobby of mine."

"Really?" said Mikki. "You mean like telling someone's future from her palm?"

"You would be amazed at how much the lines on a palm can reveal," said Mrs. Wembley. "Would you like me to show you?"

"Sure," said Mikki. She seated herself next to Mrs. Wembley on the sofa.

"Now, let me see your hands," the old woman said. She took Mikki's hands in her own and held them a moment, then took a magnifying glass from the coffee table.

Holding Mikki's right hand close to her face, she began to examine it through the magnifying glass. "Hmmmm," she said. "Mmm-hmmm . . . Oh, my."

"What do you see?" asked Mikki, half-serious. "Am I going to be successful? Will I be a famous dancer?"

For a moment Mrs. Wembley didn't answer. When she finally spoke, she sounded very solemn. "I don't see anything like that," she said. "But you will grow very old."

Mikki couldn't help laughing. "Well, I guess that's good to know," she said. "Of course, I don't really believe in that stuff."

"Don't be too sure, dear," said Mrs. Wembley calmly. "Science and logic are not the only forces in the universe. And they're certainly not the strongest!"

As Mikki was getting ready to leave, she thought over what Mrs. Wembley had said. Could the things she said be true? Maybe that really was a love potion on the stove that first day.

"Excuse me, dear," said Mrs. Wembley. "Before you go, could you get my big salad bowl down for me? It's on the top shelf."

"Of course," said Mikki. She dragged a footstool over to the kitchen area and stood on it to reach into the top cupboard. The salad bowl was in the back, and she had to take out some things from in front of it. Among the items was a metal rack holding a dozen glass vials of colored powder.

"Be careful with that!" Mrs. Wembley said sharply.

"I will," said Mikki. "Let me just set it down by the sink." She bent down to set the rack on the counter when Ha-Chee suddenly jumped up onto the same spot. Mikki saw one of the vials, filled with blue powder, tip and over-turn onto the counter.

"Oh, no!" cried Mrs. Wembley. "Look what you've done!"

"I'll clean it up," said Mikki. She wet a dishcloth at the sink and began to wipe up the powder.

"No!" cried Mrs. Wembley in a terrified voice. "You mustn't get water—"

It was too late. While Mikki watched in horror, a thick greenish fog began to rise from the cracked vial. In an instant the fog had filled the room. Mikki's eyes burned. There didn't seem to be any clean air left in the kitchen. She coughed and coughed. The room started to spin. Mikki couldn't breathe!

CHAPTER 4

MIKKI jumped off the stool and began to push on the kitchen window to let some air into the trailer. The green fog was so thick she could hardly see, and her lungs felt as if they were on fire. The room was still spinning. Ha-Chee was yowling in fright and pain, but there was no sound at all from Mrs. Wembley. By the time Mikki got the window open there were spots before her eyes.

Then, an instant later, the fog suddenly lifted. Mikki gulped in the cool, fresh air coming in through the window. When she could breathe again, she turned to help Mrs. Wembley. To her surprise the old woman seemed fine. She was calmly sprinkling the remains of a vial of red powder on the blue powder from the broken vial.

"What happened?" Mikki said, her voice a hoarse croak.

"I neutralized it," said the old lady matter-of-factly.

"What about the smoke? I thought I was going to suffocate!" cried Mikki. "What was that powder?"

"It was my fault," said Mrs. Wembley. "I should have warned you. Those powders can be very, very dangerous!"

"All I did was try to wipe it up," protested Mikki.

"Ah, but you used water," said Mrs. Wembley. "With that particular powder, adding water is like throwing an armload of dynamite on a fire."

Mikki took a step closer to the counter to get a better look at the vials. When she reached out to touch one, Mrs. Wembley suddenly shouted, "Get away from those! You don't know what you're doing!"

Shocked, Mikki jumped back. Mrs. Wembley leaned over and carefully scooped up the remaining dry blue powder and put it into an empty vial.

"What are the powders for?" Mikki asked, unable to restrain her curiosity.

Mrs. Wembley turned and gave her an odd look. "For making spells, of course," she said, as if the answer were obvious.

"Spells?" said Mikki. "What kind of spells?"

"Any kind you want," said the old woman. "Love potions, hate potions, shape-shifting potions. The one you spilled was wolfbane. That's good for a lot of different things, as long as you keep it dry." She then began to whisper some strange-sounding words as she put the vials away.

"Is this for real?" asked Mikki.

"It's for real," said Mrs. Wembley. She had a mischievous look on her face. "Would you like to help me make a spell one day?"

For a moment Mikki just stared at the old woman.

Could she *really* make spells? "I'd love to!" she answered. "Would you really let me?"

"It would be my pleasure," said Mrs. Wembley. "After all, you've done so much for me. I don't know what I'd do without you, Mikki."

Diane looked up when Mikki returned to the room, but she didn't say hello. So Mikki ignored her, too.

"Back from the toe shoe factory?" Diane finally asked as Mikki settled herself at her desk.

Mikki took a deep breath and decided to try to be nice to Diane. "I had dance this morning," Mikki said, trying to sound friendly. "I was just at my work-study with Mrs. Wembley."

"Oh, right," said Diane sarcastically. "The hundred-year-old woman who listens to Guns N' Roses."

I give up, Mikki thought. The girls spent the next hour in silence, working on their homework and not talking to each other. A little later Diane stood up and began brushing her long blond hair.

"Anita, Eric, and I are meeting in the dayroom to watch TV. Do you want to come?" Diane asked tentatively.

Mikki was so surprised that Diane was being nice that she just stared at her roommate for a second. "Thanks, but I've got to practice ballet."

"Fine, if that's what you'd rather do," said Diane. "Obviously your ballet means more to you than having friends."

Mikki was so hurt, she just stared silently at the textbook.

A few minutes later Diane tried again. "Do you like my

new sweater? My mother just sent it to me," she asked sweetly.

"It's really pretty," Mikki said truthfully. Diane had the best wardrobe of any girl at Chilleen.

"By the way," Diane said on her way out the door, "don't you think that shirt you're wearing would look better with black jeans or your cords?"

If I thought that, I would have worn them, Mikki thought, but didn't say anything. She didn't know why she even tried to be nice to Diane.

Sunday morning Mikki had rehearsal for the dance recital. As she practiced, she knew she was doing really well. Everything came together—her balance, her agility, even her leaping. When she finished, the other girls and boys on the stage applauded her.

Flushing with pride and pleasure, Mikki threw her jeans and jacket on over her leotard and went back to her room to change. She stopped outside the door, which was ajar, and listened. Diane, Anita, and Monica were all sitting on Diane's bed, giggling while Diane read to them.

" 'My rehearsal went great today,' " Diane read. " 'Sometimes when I'm up on the stage, I feel like a famous ballerina.' "

Mikki froze, hot shame flooding her body. *Diane was reading from Mikki's diary!*

"How dare you!" Mikki cried, tears filling her eyes. She was so angry that she was shaking. She rushed into the room and up to Diane. She grabbed the diary out of her hands, then ran from the room and out the front door of the academy. She didn't stop running until she was in the woods.

She sat down on a large lichen-covered rock and forced herself to take deep breaths to calm down. *How could Diane have done such a thing?* she wondered. *How could anyone be so mean? She must really hate me,* Mikki decided. *And I never did a single thing to her, except in her imagination.*

After a few minutes Mikki stood up and shoved the diary in her denim jacket pocket, then, on impulse, decided to take the bus into Silverbell. Maybe talking to Mrs. Wembley would make her feel better.

By the time she got to the trailer park she was calmer. Somehow, just thinking about seeing Mrs. Wembley cheered her up. She hurried through the weed-infested lot to the familiar battered silver trailer. As she was passing Mrs. Wembley's kitchen window, she glanced up, then stopped, curious. Mrs. Wembley was bending over her sink, deep in concentration. From the window Mikki could easily see that the object of the old woman's interest was a huge glass jar. Inside the jar was a yellowish liquid that was bubbling furiously, as if it were boiling, but there was no sign of heat or flame.

What in the world is that? Mikki wondered. *Could it be another one of her potions?* Not wanting to disturb the old woman's concentration, Mikki continued to watch. Mrs. Wembley turned away from the jar of yellow liquid to a goldfish bowl. Inside the bowl were dozens of swimming animals that looked like tadpoles. As Mikki watched, the old woman dipped a small net into the bowl and pulled out a fat, wriggling tadpole. Still using the net, she dropped the little creature into the bubbling yellow liquid.

At first nothing happened. Then the tadpole began to swim around furiously, faster and faster. And then the tadpole began to change. It seemed to get bigger, and its shape became longer. At first Mikki blinked, sure she was seeing wrong. But, no, as she watched, the little creature began to grow legs. The legs started out as tiny buds and then quickly grew longer until they were unmistakably frog legs. At the same time the tadpole's tail became shorter and shorter, and then disappeared altogether.

It was impossible, but it was happening. The tadpole was changing into a frog, right before Mikki's eyes. Its process of metamorphosis had been speeded up hundreds of times.

The window was open, and Mikki now heard a tiny *croak*. The frog jumped out of the jar and onto the sink. It wasn't through growing yet. Even though it was out of the liquid, it continued to get bigger and bigger, until it was the size of a bullfrog. It had taken less than fifteen minutes for the creature to grow from a tadpole to a frog. Then it began to change again. All at once it started to shrink, slowly at first, then faster.

As Mikki continued to watch in astonishment, the frog's skin shrunk and became dry and crinkly, like that of a mummy. Then, with a tiny *poof*, what was left of the frog crumbled to dust.

CHAPTER 5

NOT believing her eyes, Mikki continued to stare at the counter where a frog had been seconds before. All that remained of it now was a small pile of greenish dust.

What had just happened? Had she really watched a tadpole change into a frog and then disappear? But that was impossible. Unless . . . unless Mrs. Wembley really could make spells the way she said. Inside the kitchen Mrs. Wembley had begun to clean out the glass jar that had contained the bubbling liquid. Suddenly she raised her eyes and they met Mikki's.

For a moment Mikki felt as if her heart had stopped. There was an expression in the old woman's eyes she had never seen before, an expression of evil. But then, abruptly, Mrs. Wembley's face changed and she smiled.

"Is that you, Mikki dear?" she called through the window. "You know I can't see very far."

"Yes, Mrs. Wembley," said Mikki. "It's me. I'm just on my way to the door." Did Mrs. Wembley know Mikki had seen what happened with the frog? She was nervous as she entered through the front door, but Mrs. Wembley smiled as if nothing strange had happened at all.

"I guess you saw my little experiment just now," the old woman said, as casually as if she were discussing a new recipe for meat loaf.

"Was it an experiment?" Mikki blurted out. "Or a spell?"

For a moment Mrs. Wembley didn't answer, then she smiled and patted Mikki's hand. "You are very clever, dear," she said.

"But how does it work?" Mikki asked. "It looked as if the tadpole turned into a frog and then disappeared into dust."

"Yes," agreed the old woman. "Remember the other day when I told you about the powers of the universe? Well, you have witnessed them in action. Some might call it magic."

Magic. Mikki was speechless. Even though Mrs. Wembley had talked of making spells, Mikki had never quite believed that she actually had magical powers. It couldn't be, not logically. How else, though, could she have made the tadpole grow and then shrink? How could she read the future in a person's palm?

"I know it's hard to believe," said Mrs. Wembley, as if she were reading Mikki's thoughts. "But just because something *seems* impossible doesn't mean that it is."

"How long have you been able to do magic?" Mikki asked, her voice almost a croak.

"Oh, for years," said the old woman. "For more years

than you can imagine. Now, come sit on the sofa, have some tea, and tell me what's bothering you."

"How do you know something is bothering me?" asked Mikki, more spooked than ever.

The old woman laughed. "I didn't read your mind, if that's what you're thinking," she said. "No, my dear, I used simple logic. You come to see me on Tuesdays and Fridays. I know that you wouldn't come on the weekend without a very good reason."

For a moment Mikki felt the sting of tears in her eyes. "It's my roommate," she said when the old woman handed her a cup of tea. "She did something really horrible to me, and I don't know what to do about it."

Mikki began to tell Mrs. Wembley all about Diane, starting with the previous year when Mikki and Jenny and Diane had all been best friends, and finishing with how hard it was to get along with Diane as a roommate. "She won't even try to like me," Mikki told Mrs. Wembley. "No matter what I do or say, she criticizes me."

"Oh, dear," the old woman murmured. "But you said she did something horrible?"

"Yes," said Mikki. She felt herself blushing with shame as she told Mrs. Wembley about finding Diane with her diary.

"She read your private diary to her friends?" the old woman asked. She sounded shocked.

Mikki nodded. "I could hardly believe it. I didn't think even Diane could do something so mean. I just wish there were some way I could get back at her. Not hurt her, but . . . just some way to embarrass her. The way she embarrassed me today." She thought a moment, then shook her head. "But it's hopeless," she went on. "She doesn't keep a diary, and she's practically perfect, so she doesn't have anything to be embarrassed about."

"I doubt *that*," said the old woman. "Everyone has something to be embarrassed about. Stop thinking so logically, child. Free your mind from conventional thinking. Keep it open to other, wilder possibilities."

"Like what?"

"Surely you haven't forgotten what we were talking about a few moments ago?" Mrs. Wembley said.

"You mean—you mean magic?" asked Mikki.

"What else?" said Mrs. Wembley. "Serious problems call for serious remedies." She went to the bookcase and reached on tiptoe for a thin red book on the top shelf.

"What's in that book?" Mikki asked.

"Magic spells," said the old woman matter-of-factly.

"Can I see it?" asked Mikki.

"I doubt if you'll be able to read it," said Mrs. Wembley, handing it to her. "I'm afraid I've scribbled it up over the years."

Mikki took the book and leafed through it. The pages were printed in tiny, old-fashioned type, and nearly every blank space was covered with spidery blue handwriting. The leather cover was so cracked Mikki could scarcely make out the title: *Spells for Every Occasion*. "Wow," said Mikki. "This book is really old."

"Also very powerful," Mrs. Wembley said seriously. "I'm sure there's something in here that will solve the problem of Diane once and for all. I always believe in letting the punishment fit the crime. You said before that Diane is perfect. She sounds anything but perfect to me.

She sounds as if she is quite conceited. What is she most conceited about?"

"Her hair," said Mikki immediately. "She's got the most beautiful thick, long blond hair. She spends hours on it every day."

"Perfect," said the old woman, eyeing Mikki thoughtfully for a couple of minutes. "I know just what to do." She took the spell book from Mikki and went into the kitchen area. A moment later she returned with an empty glass vial and a pair of scissors. She set them on the coffee table, and then resettled herself next to Mikki. Smiling at Mikki, she announced, "We'll ruin her hair."

"Ruin her hair!" Mikki couldn't help feeling shocked. "But isn't that a little too drastic? I mean, she embarrassed me, but—"

"Relax," said Mrs. Wembley. "I told you all we'll do is embarrass her. So we'll ruin her hair for a day or two. Just long enough for her to get a taste of her own medicine. Picture it, Mikki—how would Diane feel if she woke up one morning and her hair was all kinky and frizzy and dull?"

Just like my hair, Mikki thought, unconsciously touching her own hair. She closed her eyes and pictured Diane with the same unruly, mousy-brown mop. "She'd flip out completely," Mikki said with a smile. "It would be perfect. But can we really do it?"

"You bet we can," Mrs. Wembley said. "Provided you are willing to follow my instructions."

"Well, I—" Mikki stopped to consider, then made up her mind. "I'll do whatever you say."

"Good," said the old woman. "Now lean over here."

Mikki did as she was told, and in an instant Mrs. Wembley picked up the scissors and cut off a lock of her hair. "Hey!" cried Mikki.

Quick as a whip Mrs. Wembley popped the hair into the vial. "We need your hair for the spell," she explained. "You see, we're going to turn Diane's hair into something like yours. Now, I also need a lock of her hair, and we're in business."

"Her hair?" said Mikki. "How can I get a lock of her hair?"

"I'm sure you'll think of something," said Mrs. Wembley. "If you really want to get even with her."

When Mikki got back to the academy, she was relieved that her room was empty. She took the diary out of her pocket and started to replace it in the desk drawer, then changed her mind and locked the diary in her jewelry box. She hid the key to the box in her overnight bag—a place she was sure Diane wouldn't find it.

She sat down to study but was unable to concentrate on anything but what had happened that day—Diane's stealing her diary, Mrs. Wembley's magic with the frog, and then the old woman's promise to help her get even with Diane. *If only the magic will really work.*

"Are you on a diet?" came Diane's sarcastic voice from the doorway.

"What?"

"You're going to miss supper if you just sit there," Diane went on. "Most of the other kids have already eaten."

Mikki glanced at her watch and realized that she had lost track of time. "I was just on my way," she said.

"If you're worried about my looking at your diary again, forget it," said Diane.

"As a matter of fact—" Mikki started, feeling her anger returning.

"Look, it was an accident," Diane said. "We were trying to find a pair of scissors for an art project Monica's doing. I didn't know your diary was there. I didn't even know what it was, till I started reading it."

Mikki just stared at Diane. Was that supposed to be an apology? First Diane looked through Mikki's things, and then she read the diary. How could she be so mean?

Mikki decided she would get back at Diane, and she would do it that very night!

Mikki waited until Diane's deep, regular breathing told her she was asleep, then silently crept out of her bed. She took a pair of scissors from her desk and tiptoed to Diane's bed.

Diane was lying on her back, her mouth slightly open, a beam of moonlight shining on her fair, smooth skin. Even when she was asleep, Diane looked beautiful. Her hair spilled all over her pillow and onto the bed. It was so long that Mikki thought she ought to be able to snip a lock off without Diane even noticing. She bent down, the scissors open, then suddenly jumped back as Diane shifted and turned.

A few moments later Diane was asleep again, but this time she was lying on her side, with most of her hair underneath her body. Mikki's heart was pounding furiously. She began to pull at a strand of hair, trying to work it out from under Diane. She finally freed a good-size strand and was about to snip it when Diane suddenly sat up, opening her eyes in confusion. She instantly saw Mikki, bent over her bed.

"What are you doing?" she demanded angrily. "What's going on?"

CHAPTER 6

"I—I dropped my pen," Mikki said, the first thing that came to her mind. "I think it rolled under your bed."

"Well, can't it wait till tomorrow?" Diane demanded, annoyed. "Go back to bed, will you?"

Meekly Mikki went back to her own side of the room and again waited until she could hear her roommate breathing deeply and evenly. *If it doesn't work this time, I give up,* she thought.

Even more carefully she returned to Diane's side of the room. Once again Diane's long hair was spread on the bed. One golden lock was hanging over the edge. Holding her breath, Mikki moved closer. She held out the scissors and snipped. Grinning in triumph, she slipped the hair into a plastic sandwich bag and locked it up in her jewelry box.

The next morning Mikki took the plastic bag containing Diane's hair out of her jewelry box and put it in her day pack. After what had happened to the diary, she was certainly not letting the precious hair out of her sight.

"Are you going to wear *that?*" said Diane's familiar voice as Mikki was getting ready for classes.

Mikki glanced down at her strawberry-colored shirt and faded jeans. "Why not?" she said, refusing to let Diane's criticism spoil her good mood.

"Well, it's your decision," said Diane. "But that isn't really your best color." She adjusted the belt on her own outfit, and then, with a shake of her long hair, swept out of the room.

Mikki tried not to let Diane bother her. She knew that very soon Diane wouldn't have much to feel superior about.

She was so excited she could hardly wait for Tuesday when she would see Mrs. Wembley again. At lunch Mark and his friend Eric noticed her good mood. "What's with you?" said Eric.

"Yeah, you look really up. Are you and Diane getting along better?" asked Mark.

"Not really," said Mikki. "I guess I'm just learning to live with her."

"Guess what," Mark said. "For my work-study I'm going to be stage manager for the dance recital."

"Really?" said Mikki. "How'd you get that?"

"Well, you know I've always been interested in acting," said Mark. "But all the work-study jobs in the drama department were taken for this semester. So I asked to be made stage manager for the recital instead."

"That's great, Mark," said Mikki. "It'll be good to have a friend there during rehearsals."

That afternoon during dance practice, Mikki worked hard to perfect her solo. It wasn't her first solo, but it was the biggest one she'd ever had. She knew if she did well she'd have a good chance of getting the lead in the spring ballet. She knew she was dancing her best, and was happy to hear Mark clap when she finished.

The following afternoon she double-checked to make sure Diane's hair was still in the plastic bag before boarding the bus to Silverbell. Mrs. Wembley was wearing a green sweatshirt with her yellow stretch pants and had the CD player blaring when Mikki arrived.

As always, the old woman beamed as soon as she saw Mikki. "Come in, dear," she said. "Let me just turn down the music." Mikki was about to tell Mrs. Wembley about the lock of Diane's hair, but before she could get a word out, Mrs. Wembley put a hand on her arm. "I got a new book from the bookmobile today. Another vampire book," she told Mikki, sounding excited. "It's in the bedroom. Would you mind getting it?"

Mikki felt sympathy for the old woman. She couldn't imagine being so feeble. Mikki went into the bedroom, which was behind the kitchen, and found the book lying on the bed. On the way out of the room her eye caught a group of photographs along a shelf. Curious, she stopped to glance at them. There was an old, yellowed picture of a young woman dressed in a long hoop skirt with her hair pulled back in a tight bun. The kind of photos that were taken during the Civil War. The young woman was holding a cat that looked like Ha-Chee. Then Mikki realized that the young woman looked a lot like Mrs. Wembley must have when she was young. *It must be her grandmother or great-grandmother*, she thought. *How strange that she had a cat that looked exactly like the one Mrs. Wembley has now.*

Next to the picture of Mrs. Wembley's grandmother was a larger frame containing three photos of three young girls about Mikki's age. All of the girls were from different time periods. One of them was wearing a long dress, apron, and bonnet; another had on a long ruffled skirt, very puffy sleeves, high-button shoes, and white gloves; and the third was dressed in a poodle skirt, bobby socks, and saddle shoes. None of them resembled Mrs. Wembley in the least, and Mikki wondered if they were distant relatives.

"Mikki?" Mrs. Wembley's voice broke into the girl's thoughts. "Are you having trouble finding the book?"

"Sorry," said Mikki, coming back into the living room. "I was looking at your family pictures."

"There's a lot of history in those pictures," said Mrs. Wembley.

"Who are the three girls in the frame on the end?" Mikki asked. "The ones in the old-fashioned clothes?"

"Oh, they're just some girls who . . . helped me out in the past," said Mrs. Wembley.

Mikki hid a smile. Probably Mrs. Wembley had forgotten who the girls were. "I liked the picture of your grandmother," she said. "Or was it your great-grandmother? The one holding the cat."

"That's not my grandmother," said Mrs. Wembley, sounding annoyed. "That was me, when I was as young as you are."

Right, thought Mikki, but she didn't say anything. Mrs. Wembley couldn't help it if she got confused about time.

"Before I start reading," Mikki said, "I wanted to tell you I got that lock of my roommate's hair."

"You did!" said the old woman. "Well, why didn't you say so before?" She got up from the sofa and disappeared into the kitchen area. When she came back, she had two vials with her. One contained the lock of hair that she had cut from Mikki's head, the other a half inch of bluish powder.

"Do you think this spell will really work?" Mikki asked the old woman.

Mrs. Wembley appeared to be insulted. "Of course it will!" she said. "Magic follows natural laws just like science. The only thing that could ruin the spell is if you insist on being skeptical. These things work best when you believe they will work."

"I'm sorry," said Mikki. "It's just so strange to think about."

"In these days perhaps," grumbled Mrs. Wembley. "But there was a time not so long ago when everyone knew about the powers of the universe." She squinted at the two vials in her hands, then opened the one with Mikki's hair and placed exactly three strands in the vial with the powder. "Now give me your roommate's hair," she instructed.

Mikki passed it over and watched as Mrs. Wembley removed the long golden hair from the bag. She took three strands of Diane's hair and added it to the vial with Mikki's hair and the powder. Then she put the rest of Diane's hair in the first vial with Mikki's hair.

"Are three hairs enough?" Mikki asked, fascinated.

"More than enough," said Mrs. Wembley. "For most spells one hair is enough. I put in three just to make sure."

"Wow," said Mikki. "What are you going to do with the rest of it?"

"I'll just throw it away," said Mrs. Wembley. "Don't worry about it. Now," she went on quickly, "I want you to listen to me very carefully. In fact, you should probably make notes. Because if the spell is to work, you must follow my instructions *exactly*. Do you understand?"

"Yes," said Mikki.

"Good," said Mrs. Wembley. She opened the thin red-covered spell book. Then, using her magnifying glass, she began to read Mikki instructions for the spell. Mikki listened carefully, making notes. Occasionally she stopped and asked Mrs. Wembley to repeat herself because the instructions were so complicated and strange.

"Have you got all that?" asked the old woman when she had finished.

"I think so," said Mikki.

"Good," said Mrs. Wembley. "The spell will last for exactly twenty-four hours, which should be long enough to convince your roommate that she is not perfect."

"I can't wait," said Mikki, stifling a giggle.

"You'll need to do it soon," Mrs. Wembley went on. "The power of the powder will begin to fade after a few days."

"I know exactly when to do it," said Mikki. "This Thursday night. Then her hair will be wrecked for Friday, which just happens to be the day of our class pictures."

"That sounds perfect," said Mrs. Wembley. "I promise I'll be thinking of you Thursday night."

For the next couple days Mikki had to force herself to concentrate on her schoolwork. She was so excited she could hardly wait for Friday. She imagined Diane's face when she saw what had happened to her hair. Even better, Diane would have to be in the school yearbook with frizzy hair. Mikki was afraid she would give away something because of her excitement, so she did most of her studying in the dayroom and library with Mark and Ellen.

When she returned to her room from studying Thursday night, Diane was already sitting on her bed in her pajamas, brushing her long, beautiful, soon-to-be-frizzy hair. "Where've you been?" Diane asked, sounding almost friendly.

"Oh, around," Mikki said vaguely. "I've been busy."

"Oh, right, I forgot," said Diane, once again sounding like Diane. "Toe shoes and old folks."

"What've you been up to?" asked Mikki, not really caring.

"Oh, the usual," said Diane. "Playing volleyball and studying. I'm pretty sure I'm going to make mostly all A's this semester."

"Good for you," said Mikki. She sat on her bed and untied her sneakers. "Well," she said casually, "are you all ready for the school pictures tomorrow?"

"Of course I am," said Diane. "I have my clothes all picked out. Mom sent me a new pink blouse—it's a perfect color for me."

"Sounds great," said Mikki, imagining the pink blouse with frizzy, mousy hair.

"Want me to help you pick out an outfit?" Diane offered.

Is she trying to be helpful? Mikki wondered. *Or is this another put-down?* "No, thanks," she said. "I already know what I'll wear." She did a few ballet stretches and changed into her robe. "See you later," she said. "I'm going to go brush my teeth."

At eleven o'clock Mikki sat up and glanced over at Diane, who had gone to bed shortly after ten. Mikki had stayed up a while longer, pretending to study but really reading over the instructions for the spell, which had to be memorized.

Mrs. Wembley had told her the spell must be done at exactly 11:11, so Mikki had pretended to go to sleep but actually kept her eye on the clock all the time.

She slipped on her sneakers and put a jacket on over her nightgown. Then, taking the vial, she crept out the door and down the stairs. The old Chilleen mansion was silent, and Mikki quietly unlatched the front door before stepping out into the cool night. The moon was full and so bright that the pine trees cast shadows nearly as sharp as during the day. She stepped onto the front lawn, then began to search for a clear beam of moonlight.

She found one by the photo shed behind the main academy building. She stood in the shadows holding the vial until the time was right. According to her watch it was 11:08. Only three more minutes.

Taking a deep breath, she moved forward into the light and started to pull the stopper out of the vial. Just at that

46

moment she heard a sharp snapping noise, and then a bright light shone in her eyes, blinding her.

With a small shriek Mikki jumped back in the shadows, but the light followed her.

"Who's there?" came a familiar, gruff voice. It was Mr. Fernandez, the night watchman.

"It's me," Mikki said. "Mikki Merrill."

"What are you doing out here at this hour?" said Mr. Fernandez, sounding astonished. "It's way past lights-out."

"I know," Mikki told him, thinking fast. "But I—I need to collect some night-crawling caterpillars for a science project."

"In the middle of the night?" asked Mr. Fernandez in disbelief.

"It's the only time they come out," said Mikki. "Look," she added, thrusting the vial at him. "The science teacher gave me this to catch them in."

"Well, I don't know," said Mr. Fernandez, barely glancing at the vial.

Please, Mikki thought. *Please leave me alone.* If he didn't go away it was going to be too late to do the spell. "I promise I'll go in as soon as I get a caterpillar," Mikki pleaded. "In fact, I was on the track of one when you showed up. It was right over there in the grass."

"All right," said Mr. Fernandez, moving off. "But you go on inside as soon as you finish," he called back to her.

"I promise," said Mikki. She glanced at her watch. 11:11. Not even stopping to review the spell, she stepped into the patch of moonlight. Then, as Mrs. Wembley had instructed, she shut her eyes and held the vial to her lips.

Then she reached into it and took a pinch of the bluish powder from inside.

"Oh-ma-na-cliru-sclee!" she said, repeating the strange, foreign words she had memorized. She sprinkled a few grains of the powder on her head, then turned till she was facing north. *"Oh-ma-na-cliru-sclee!"* she repeated and tossed a bit of the powder toward the north.

Slowly she turned again until she was facing south and repeated the words while she sprinkled more of the powder. Next, she turned east, then west. When she had finished, there was only a little powder left in the vial. She didn't know if she was supposed to use up all the powder. She wondered if she should sprinkle the rest of it, but Mrs. Wembley had been insistent that she follow the instructions to the letter.

Mikki had replaced the stopper in the vial and started to walk inside when she noticed a strange feeling at the top of her head. It was kind of a warm tingling, a bit like an electric shock, but not painful. In fact, it was rather pleasant. The tingling moved down her head to her neck and then spread to her shoulders, her arms, her fingertips. By the time she reached the front porch, her whole body was throbbing with the strange tingling.

It's working, Mikki realized with a mixture of disbelief and excitement. *The spell is working!*

CHAPTER 7

THE tingling began to fade when Mikki reached her room. In its place was a warm, relaxed feeling. She wondered what it meant. Was it really magic? Did Mrs. Wembley really have special powers? She couldn't believe that the spell was actually working!

She was too excited to go back to bed right then. She wished she knew how long the spell took to change hair. She tiptoed over to Diane's bed and peered at her. For now her hair was still beautiful and shiny. *Just wait till tomorrow,* Mikki thought, satisfied. *Wait till you see what your hair looks like when you wake up!*

The next morning Mikki overslept. When she finally did wake up, she stretched and yawned, still sleepy and a little achy. And then she remembered what had happened the night before. *I stayed up too late,* she realized.

It was going to be worth it, though. She glanced over at Diane's bed, but Diane had already gotten up. Mikki was disappointed; she had hoped to be the first to see Diane's new frizzy hair. She wondered where her roommate was. She couldn't wait to see her!

She pulled on her robe and padded down the hall to the shower room. She still felt unusually sleepy and hoped a shower would wake her up.

A few girls were in the shower room, most of them dressed and ready to go down to breakfast. "Hi, Mikki," said Monica Case, with toothpaste in her mouth. "Are you just getting up?"

"I guess I overslept," said Mikki.

"Are you all right?" said Monica. "You look a little tired."

Mikki peered into the mirror and saw that Monica was right. She was pale and had dark circles under her eyes. She promised herself she would go to bed extra early that night. "I stayed up too late last night," she said. "Have you seen Diane today?"

"Your roommate?" said Monica. "No, do you want me to give her a message if I see her?"

"No," said Mikki. "It's nothing. See you later."

She stepped into the shower stall and turned the water on full blast, letting its wet warmth sting her awake. *I can't wait till they take the school pictures,* she thought. *What will Diane do? Maybe she'll wear a bag over her head!*

Then she had another thought: *What if the spell didn't work?* Mikki calmed herself. Hadn't she felt the weird tingling the night before when she had sprinkled the powder and said the strange words? It must have been the magic working. But the only way to find out for sure, she realized, was to find Diane. She turned off the water and began to dry off, rubbing herself all over with a fluffy towel.

She was just about to slip her robe back on when a piercing scream rang through the shower room. "Oh, no!" cried Diane's familiar voice. "My hair is ruined!"

CHAPTER 8

*I*T *worked!* Mikki thought happily. *The spell worked and Diane's hair is going to look terrible in the class picture!*

She quickly slipped on her robe and rushed out of the shower area. Three girls were standing at one of the sinks in the corner. The girl in the middle was Diane. She was hidden from Mikki's view by Monica and the other girl, Diane's good friend Anita.

"It's ruined!" Diane wailed again. "How can I possibly have my picture taken?"

"Calm down," said Anita, who was always cool and collected no matter what.

"How can I?" said Diane. "Just look at my hair."

"Most people would be thrilled if they had hair like yours," said Monica. "Somehow I think your picture will be just fine." Diane started to turn away, and now Mikki could see her clearly.

"Imagine how she would look with mousy, frizzy, dull hair," Mrs. Wembley had said. For a moment that's just

what Mikki saw. Then she realized that it was her imagination. From the back, at least, Diane's hair was as shiny, thick, and perfect as ever. Mikki felt a lump of disappointment rising in her throat.

"Don't be so conceited," Anita was saying to Diane. "There's nothing wrong with your hair. You just slept on it a little funny. I can fix it in a minute with some hair spray."

Mikki continued to stare at Diane. Now she could see that there was a cowlick sticking up on one side, from where Diane had slept on her hair wrong.

"Give me that," Diane said irritably, taking the hair spray from Anita. Angrily she began to spray the cowlick as if it were a large bug she were trying to poison. Then she saw Mikki's reflection in the mirror.

"What are you staring at?" she demanded, spinning around to glare at Mikki.

"Nothing," said Mikki, taken aback. "I was just in the shower room."

"Well, you shouldn't be spying on me!" Diane said. She returned to working on her already perfect hair. Mikki was angry as she made her way back to their room.

Her anger quickly vanished and was replaced by sadness. The spell hadn't worked, she realized. There wasn't any magic after all. Mrs. Wembley wasn't a magician, she was just a kooky old lady.

By the time of the class picture, Mikki still felt tired and disappointed. She knew her picture was going to look awful. Diane, of course, looked as if she had just stepped off the cover of a fashion magazine. Mikki watched jealously as Diane settled herself in the front row and flashed her million-dollar smile. *How could Mrs. Wembley do this to me?* she wondered. *How could she claim to be able to do something she couldn't?*

Then she remembered the tadpole that had turned into a frog. *Maybe Mrs. Wembley can only do certain kinds of spells*, Mikki thought. *Maybe she isn't as good at magic as she used to be. Or maybe she just had me go through all that to cheer me up. And, come to think of it, it* did *cheer me up for a couple of days.*

Mikki wasn't feeling well that afternoon and skipped her visit to Mrs. Wembley. When she visited the following Tuesday, Mikki found the old woman squatting in the weed-filled flower bed at the front of her trailer.

"Hello, Mikki," Mrs. Wembley said. "It's such a beautiful day I thought I'd get a little exercise."

"That's good," said Mikki distractedly. "I know it's usually hard for you to bend over." She held out a hand to help Mrs. Wembley to her feet, but the old woman didn't seem to want her help.

Mrs. Wembley wiped the dirt off her hands, then turned to her and frowned. "Mikki, what's wrong?"

"Oh, Mrs. Wembley," Mikki blurted out. "The spell didn't work. The morning of the class pictures Diane's hair was as beautiful as ever."

"That's too bad," said Mrs. Wembley, opening the trailer door. "Usually that's one of the most reliable spells I know. Maybe you didn't do it right."

"At first I thought I'd done something wrong," Mikki said. "But then I checked over your instructions, and I followed them exactly."

"Well, there's nothing I can tell you. You did it *wrong*." Mrs. Wembley turned her back to Mikki and busied herself at the bookshelf.

Mikki sat on the couch, upset and depressed. She couldn't believe how uncaring Mrs. Wembley seemed.

"Don't get upset. I don't blame you," said Mrs. Wembley. "Magic can be very unpredictable, didn't I tell you that?"

"No," said Mikki. "Why is that?"

"I suppose it has to do with the powers of the universe," Mrs. Wembley said. "Sometimes a spell doesn't work at all, or sometimes it gives you the wrong result. I remember once when I was trying to transform a man I know into a frog, but all that happened was he grew taller."

"Are you serious?" Mikki just stared at the old woman.

"To this day I don't know what went wrong," Mrs. Wembley continued, as if she were talking about a mistake she'd made in a cake recipe. "I double-checked the powders, and the words of the spell. It was just one of those things."

"I guess what happened with Diane was—was another one," said Mikki.

"We'll try the same spell again next month at the same time," Mrs. Wembley said briskly. "And I'm sure it will work then." She picked up her new vampire book from the coffee table. "Let's start reading," she said.

The next morning Mikki had a geography quiz, and for the second time in a week she slept through her alarm and almost missed the class. *What's the matter with me?*

she thought. She knew the answer—she was doing too much. That's what her mother would tell her: "Slow down, honey, you don't need to do everything at once."

She realized that there was some truth to that. She had always been a good student, and maybe she was working harder than usual this semester to make sure she got better grades than Diane. In fact, she'd been up quite late studying for the quiz. In addition to her regular schoolwork and her work for Mrs. Wembley, she was also busy practicing long hours for the dance recital.

Mikki quickly put on a pair of jeans, which were thrown on her chair, and a sweatshirt. She ran to the mirror to brush her hair. She had only a few minutes to get to her class. As she focused in on her reflection, Mikki stopped brushing and gasped in disbelief.

Right in the center of her head was a long wiry strand of *gray* hair!

She couldn't believe she was getting gray hairs already. It seemed so ridiculous that Mikki almost laughed aloud. She immediately yanked the gray hair out of her head and put on a purple baseball cap.

Mikki only had time to grab a piece of toast before running to her first-period geography class. By the time she slipped into her seat, she was out of breath. When the teacher passed out photocopies of the quiz, she found she had to squint to read the letters. They were so tiny they seemed to dance before her eyes. *The teacher must have gotten a new typewriter*, Mikki thought. *I wonder why she got one with such small print?* Luckily, Mikki had no trouble at all answering the test questions. She left the classroom certain that she had aced it.

By the end of the day she wasn't feeling well at all. Every joint in her body seemed to ache. *How am I going to dance?* she wondered. To her relief Mrs. Braine, the dance instructor, spent most of the session on the girls and boys who were dancing in the chorus.

"How you doing, Mikki?" Mark asked her as she stood on the sidelines watching the other dancers.

"Okay," said Mikki, "but I'm glad I don't have to do my routine today. For some reason I'm really pooped, and my knees are kind of achy."

"Maybe you ought to put ice on them," said Mark. "Don't forget that we're having our first dress rehearsal next week."

For some reason Mikki *had* forgotten about the dress rehearsal. "Are you sure?" she said.

"Don't you remember?" said Mark. "Mrs. Braine told us about it yesterday."

How could I have forgotten something so important? Mikki wondered. *Maybe I really ought to slow down for a few days.*

Two days later she felt achier than ever. Mikki considered spending the day in bed but knew she had dance rehearsal and classes. Also she was looking forward to seeing Mrs. Wembley.

As always, approaching Mrs. Wembley's trailer, Mikki immediately felt cheerier and more energetic. It was a beautiful day, and the old woman had the front door of the trailer propped open to catch the soft fall breeze.

Mikki knocked lightly and was about to step on in, certain that as usual the old woman wouldn't hear her. To her surprise Mrs. Wembley looked up right away. "Mikki, what do you want?" she asked, not seeming too pleased to see her. She had an old pair of gold-rimmed spectacles perched on her nose and a magazine in her lap.

Mikki stared at the old woman in disbelief. "This is the day I always come. What—what are you reading?"

Mrs. Wembley touched the glasses and pushed them up on top of her head. "I found these old spectacles when I was cleaning out some drawers," she said. "So I tried them on and found I could read with them."

"Well, that's great," said Mikki. *And strange*, she thought. The last time she'd seen Mrs. Wembley, she'd been practically blind. "Maybe I ought to try them," she joked. "I've been having trouble reading lately."

"You've probably been studying too much," the old woman said and went back to reading her magazine.

"Maybe," said Mikki. "But I haven't been feeling well at all."

"You know, I've heard there's a bug going around. One of those new kinds of flu," Mrs. Wembley said. "I understand the symptoms are just what you're describing. Tiredness and blurred vision."

That must be what it is, Mikki thought with relief. *I've picked up a bug. It can't last too long, can it?*

When Mikki returned to her room at the academy, she decided to skip studying and just go to bed. She felt totally run-down. Diane was in the dayroom watching television, so Mikki knew the room would be quiet. She changed into her nightgown, put on a robe, and went down the hall to the bathroom to wash up.

THE SPELL

Mikki stood at the sink in front of the mirror, rinsing the soap off her face. She raised her head and saw a sight so incredible, so *horrifying*, that goose bumps rose on her skin and she had trouble breathing. She wanted to scream but knew she shouldn't. Mikki couldn't believe this was happening to her.

In the exact place where she had pulled out the single gray hair, *four* new gray hairs had appeared!

CHAPTER 9

WHEN Mikki woke Saturday morning, she prayed that the gray hairs would be gone. That it was all her imagination. That they were just some freak of nature. One glance in the mirror and Mikki got that same tight feeling in her chest. Now there were six gray hairs. Two more had grown overnight! She didn't know what she was going to do. She didn't want to be the world's youngest gray-haired girl. But she didn't know how to stop it. To make matters worse, her skin was beginning to feel unusually itchy and dry.

Even Ellen noticed that she wasn't herself.

The girls were sitting in the library, studying for an algebra quiz. "I can never do these word problems," Ellen complained. "If a plane starts flying from New York at three hundred miles an hour and another plane starts flying from San Francisco at two hundred fifty miles an hour, and the distance between them is thirty-five hundred miles, how long does it take them to meet?"

"Let's see," said Mikki, writing down the numbers. "How far apart did you say they are?"

Ellen repeated the numbers.

"Well, what you do," said Mikki—and then she stopped. She couldn't remember what to do. "Let's go back to the sample problems," she said, suddenly worried. Just last week she'd been able to do word problems easily. Now she hadn't a clue how to begin.

"Are you okay?" Ellen suddenly asked.

"Why?"

"You look sort of—I don't know," said Ellen, "upset. You have all these lines on your face."

"What do you mean?"

"Worry lines," said Ellen. "Maybe you ought to go back to your room and take a nap. I'm sure you'll feel better."

Going back to her room, Mikki felt a sense of rising panic. *What's happening to me?* she wondered. *What's wrong?* She lay on her bed and began to think about it. Then she realized that she'd felt fine when she'd started school and for the first couple of weeks. Her troubles had started sometime after she began working for Mrs. Wembley. Had she caught some sort of bug from her?

Suddenly she remembered all the strange chemicals the old woman used for her spells. Most of them smelled terrible, and Mrs. Wembley herself had pointed out that some of them were dangerous. *Maybe,* Mikki thought, *I'm allergic to them.* She hoped this whole thing was just some sort of strange allergic reaction.

On Monday Mikki still felt strange and went to the school nurse. The nurse, not sure what was wrong, sent Mikki into Silverbell to see Dr. Johnson.

"You seem a little run-down," Dr. Johnson told Mikki. He and Mikki were sitting in his office after the physical exam. The doctor, a tall, thin, gray-haired man, was writing notes on her chart. "I can't find anything really wrong with you," he said. "I'm going to recommend that you start taking vitamins. And you should make an appointment with Dr. Harrelson, the eye doctor."

"Eye doctor?" said Mikki.

"Your eye exam shows that you need glasses," the doctor said. "Nothing to worry about, it's perfectly normal for girls your age."

Mikki left the doctor's office more depressed than ever. Glasses. She was going to have to wear glasses. Her eyesight had always been perfect. *But why couldn't he find out what's wrong with me?* she wondered. The doctor hadn't agreed with Mikki's theory that she was having an allergic reaction. He also didn't think gray hairs were anything to worry about.

On an impulse, she decided to stop at Mrs. Wembley's before taking the bus back to school. Seeing the old woman always cheered her up.

That day Mrs. Wembley seemed preoccupied. "Why, Mikki," she said, "what a surprise." She didn't look as if she thought it was a good surprise, and Mikki turned to go.

"I'm sorry," Mikki said. "I can see you're busy. I'll come back tomorrow."

"No, no," said the old woman. "As long as you're here, you might as well come in for a cup of tea."

Mikki followed Mrs. Wembley into the trailer. There were boxes of linens and books on the floor. "I'm just sorting through a few things," Mrs. Wembley explained. She leaned down and picked up a large, heavy box.

"Can I help you with that?" Mikki asked.

"No, thanks," said Mrs. Wembley. "I can manage." She put the box on the table, then went to the kitchen area and began to prepare tea. *I can't believe it,* Mikki thought. *Just a few weeks ago she could hardly bend down, let alone lift a heavy box.*

"Mikki, clear off that table so we can have tea!" Mrs. Wembley shouted from the kitchen. It sounded more like a command than a request.

"Now," said Mrs. Wembley, returning with the tea, "sit down and tell me what your problem is."

Trying not to sound sorry for herself, Mikki told Mrs. Wembley about how bad she'd been feeling and about finding the gray hairs. "The doctor says there isn't anything wrong," she finished, "but I know there is. I keep thinking that it might have something to do with—with your chemicals."

"What are you talking about?" Mrs. Wembley asked sharply.

"You know," said Mikki. "All those powders and things you keep in the vials. I keep thinking I must be allergic to them."

"Don't be ridiculous," said Mrs. Wembley, her voice even more unfriendly. "There's nothing wrong with those powders, and they have nothing to do with the way you're feeling. The truth, young lady, is that you're trying to do too many things at once and you're overtired."

Maybe, Mikki thought, but it felt like more than that.

"Now, Mikki," Mrs. Wembley said, "go get me my glasses. They're in the bedroom."

Mikki couldn't believe the change in Mrs. Wembley. The old woman used to be so friendly. Mikki got up and walked slowly into the bedroom. She had to look around a bit before she found the glasses. They were sitting on the shelf right next to the old pictures of the three girls. Mikki glanced again at the photos and saw something she hadn't noticed before. *That's strange,* she thought. *The armchair all three girls were posed next to looked exactly like the one Mrs. Wembley had in her living room.*

"Mikki!" Mrs. Wembley's voice jolted her out of her thoughts. She returned to the living room.

"What took so long?" asked the old woman.

"I had trouble finding them," answered Mikki. She was about to ask Mrs. Wembley some questions about the strange photographs when the old woman suddenly said, "Can you do me a favor?"

"Sure," answered Mikki. "What is it?"

"I want a photograph to remember you by. It will only take a minute." Mrs. Wembley held up a small camera.

Too puzzled to speak, Mikki just stood where she was.

"Please, dear, could you move over by the armchair?" Mrs. Wembley gently guided her over to the chair. *Why does she want me by the armchair?* thought Mikki. *Just like those other girls.*

"Now, say 'cheese,' " said the old woman. "I want to see that fresh young smile."

On the bus ride back to Chilleen, Mikki couldn't figure out what was going on with Mrs. Wembley. She had definitely changed. The old woman had started to make Mikki nervous. She just wished she knew why.

The dress rehearsal for the dance recital was that night after dinner, and Mikki hadn't had the time or energy to practice the last few days. She had practiced it dozens of times in the past and was sure she'd be able to get through it.

When she began warming up, her knees started aching again. She could scarcely bend over to touch the floor. *What's wrong with me?* she wondered again.

Mrs. Braine began playing the piano, and on cue Mikki stepped out onto the stage and began her dance. It was the biggest role she'd ever had, and as always when she was performing, she gave it her full concentration. As the familiar music played on she got more and more into it. She thought she was doing well when Mrs. Braine suddenly stopped playing. "Mikki," the teacher demanded, "what's the matter with you?"

"What do you mean?" asked Mikki, shocked.

"You're a beat or two behind your music," said the older woman, "and your form seems off. Are you feeling all right?"

"I'm a little tired," Mikki admitted, "but I feel all right. Let's go through it again from the beginning."

"Very well," the teacher said and started playing again. Mikki concentrated harder than she ever had on anything in her life. *One, two, three, plié,* she told herself. *Dip, dip, turn, jump.* She sneaked a glance at Mrs. Braine and got an approving look. She continued to push herself as the music moved faster and faster. In just a moment she'd go into her final moves, a series of fast spins. As the final music began, Mikki launched herself into them, focusing on a single point out in the auditorium, snapping her head around with each turn to keep the spot in focus.

Then, suddenly, her vision began to blur. She couldn't see her spot. A second after that she couldn't even see the stage. Everything appeared to be covered with a thick fog. Her spins were supposed to take her from the center to the very edge of the stage, but where was the edge?

Not sure where to put her foot, she reached out, trying to feel where to stop the spins. Then, suddenly, through the fog, she heard frightened screams. The next thing she knew, her foot was hanging in midair and she was falling off the stage.

CHAPTER 10

MIKKI's heart was beating wildly. She twisted, trying to grab on to something to break her fall. There was nothing to hold onto, and she landed in a heap on the floor just in front of the auditorium seats.

"Mikki!" She could hear Mrs. Braine's voice above those of the other students'. Shaken and frightened, Mikki looked up to see them all crowded around her.

"Don't move," said Mrs. Braine sharply.

Mikki could tell that she wasn't seriously hurt. "I'm all right," she said. There was a sharp pain in her wrist, but she moved her hand back and forth and could tell nothing was broken. "I'm all right," she told the teacher and her friends. "Honest. I just got a little dizzy."

"You're pale as a sheet," said the teacher. "I think you should see the nurse."

"Maybe so," said Mikki. "Only can't we just get back to the rehearsal?"

"Not today," said Mrs. Braine kindly but firmly. "Not after what just happened. We'll continue with Linda for today."

Mikki couldn't believe her ears. Linda Davidson was her understudy. She would dance the solo if Mikki couldn't do it. "Please," Mikki said. "Please let me continue."

"Not today," said Mrs. Braine gently. "Besides, Linda needs the practice time, too."

After being told by the nurse to go directly to bed, Mikki returned to her room. Diane was there.

As usual, her roommate studied Mikki critically. "Your skin's looking awfully splotchy," Diane said in her usual "helpful" way. "Have you been out in the sun a lot lately?"

"I always wear sunscreen," said Mikki.

"Well, you need something more than that," said Diane. "Here, try my new Super-spectra nightcream."

Why do all Diane's offers of help feel like insults? Mikki wondered. Still, her skin was so dry it was driving her crazy. "Thanks," she said, taking some of the cream. After a few minutes her skin *did* feel better, but it was still splotchy.

"You know," said Diane, "I don't think you've been taking care of yourself lately."

"Thanks a lot," Mikki said. She was in no mood to deal with Diane.

"I'm just trying to help," said Diane. "I think you'd look a lot better if you'd just spend more time on yourself. You never did use that conditioner on your hair, did you?"

"No, I didn't," Mikki admitted.

"Well, if I were you I'd think about doing it," Diane said. "Your hair's always looked a bit dull, but it's getting so bad, if I didn't know better, I'd think you were turning gray."

Mikki sat on her bed and put her head in her hands. She tried not to cry. What in the world was happening to her? She had never gotten dizzy and lost her balance like that while dancing. She had to get reading glasses. She had no energy anymore. And to top it off, her hair was definitely turning gray. *I'm losing control of my own body*, thought Mikki with horror.

Mikki's dreams that night were a confused jumble of images: Mrs. Wembley, the dance rehearsal, school. She began to dream that she was going on a long journey, over mountains and deep into valleys. She didn't know where she was going, only that she had to keep walking. She could feel the cold ground and pine needles beneath her feet, brambles and vines cutting her bare ankles as she moved through the forest.

At last she reached a long road that stretched off into blackness. She began to make her way along the road, following the dotted white line that ran down its center. She continued to walk, unable to stop. Suddenly two lights appeared before her. The lights grew bigger and bigger, closer and closer, and Mikki realized they were headlights. The headlights of a truck.

She also realized that they were real. She wasn't dreaming! She was walking down deserted highway in the middle of the night with a large truck bearing down on her.

CHAPTER 11

FREEZING in terror, Mikki watched as the huge semi-trailer continued to speed toward her.

Closer the truck came. Closer. When the driver saw her, he leaned on his air horn. The howl of the horn filled the night darkness, and it jolted Mikki awake and gave her sudden strength.

With a terrified lurch, she threw herself onto the shoulder of the road, just as the truck rolled past the spot where she had been standing. She could feel the rush of air as it sped by.

Her heart pounding, she lay by the side of the road until her terror began to go away and her heartbeat returned to normal. She looked around her and saw that she had been walking on the Silverbell Road, the highway that led from the school to Silverbell. It would be easy to get there from school.

How had she gotten there, though? *Did I sleepwalk?* she wondered. She'd never done such a thing in her life.

Still trembling, she picked herself up and dusted off her nightgown. She started following the road back to school when something jumped out in front of her and howled. Mikki stepped back with a shriek as she recognized the animal.

It was Ha-Chee, Mrs. Wembley's cat. There was no question at all. She'd never seen another cat like it in her life.

"Ha-Chee?" she asked, her voice quavering. The little animal arched its back and spit at her, then began running along the road in the opposite direction, toward Silverbell. Mikki stared after Ha-Chee for a moment, her mind turning furiously. Ha-Chee must have followed her. Somehow, the cat knew she would be out on the Silverbell Road. That meant—the only thing it could mean was that her troubles had something to do with Mrs. Wembley.

Luckily the red-dirt road leading to the academy wasn't far, and Mikki reminded herself that she'd made this walk before in the daylight. She'd never done it at night, though, and had never realized how dark the forest was, how eerie. All around her she could hear the rustlings and stirrings of night animals—the hoot of an owl, the howling of a coyote. To either side of her along the road she heard footsteps. She began to walk faster. *Don't scare yourself, Mikki*, she told herself. *It's just a forest. They're just animals*.

Then she heard something louder, a heavy crunching and then a loud snarl. *What was it?* she wondered. *A mountain lion? A bear? Or something worse?* From the sound it was just ahead of her, to one side of the path. For a moment she thought she could see eyes, glowing yellow in the darkness. She had never believed the stories about Phantom Valley, but then she had never believed in magic, either. The creature, whatever it was, snarled again, and Mikki broke into a run. By the time she reached the broad front lawn of the academy, she was exhausted, gasping for air.

She was almost to the porch when something dark flew above her head, then swooped down at her, coming closer. She shrieked and began to run faster. The thing swooped at her again and again, giving off a high-pitched squeal. From the corner of her eye she could see it was a bat. She darted across the lawn, then finally stumbled up onto the porch. The bat swooped one final time, then flew off into the night. It was, she realized with relief, just hunting insects.

Not even thinking, she put her hand on the doorknob to turn it. To her great relief, it was unlocked. She must have left it open when she left. Inside the hall she stood leaning against the closed door for a moment, waiting for the beating of her heart to slow down. Now all she had to do was get up to her room without being seen. She looked down the hall and in the dayroom, but there was no sign of Mr. Fernandez. Probably he was making his rounds outside.

Despite her fatigue, she had trouble falling asleep. Her mind kept filling with the picture of the truck. *I could have been killed*, she realized. *At the very least I could have gotten hurt*. Much as she hated to think it, she was sure that what had happened had to do with Mrs. Wembley. The next day was one of her regular days with the old woman. No matter what, she decided, she was going to confront Mrs. Wembley and find out just what was going on.

"Hi, Mrs. Wembley," Mikki said. "You look great today."

"Why, thank you," said Mrs. Wembley. "Do you really think so?"

"I've never seen you so—so young looking," Mikki said truthfully. Mrs. Wembley's skin seemed to have lost most of its wrinkles, and her hair was more brown than white. *She looks so energetic and healthy*, Mikki thought sadly. *Just the opposite of me.*

"What about you?" Mrs. Wembley asked. "You're still looking a little tired."

"I am," Mikki admitted, "and that's not all. I have to talk to you about something really serious."

"Oh, dear," said Mrs. Wembley. "Can't it wait?"

"I don't think so," said Mikki. She took a deep breath. How was she going to say this? "Mrs. Wembley," she finally said, "some really strange things have been happening to me lately."

"Is it that dreary roommate of yours again?" asked Mrs. Wembley.

"This doesn't have anything to do with Diane," Mikki said. "But you know I haven't been feeling well, and I had an accident while I was dancing, and then last night I almost got run over on the Silverbell Road."

"What in the world are you talking about?" asked Mrs. Wembley.

Trying to speak calmly and rationally, Mikki told Mrs.

Wembley what had happened the previous night, including seeing Ha-Chee. The old lady didn't seem to be listening to her.

"You obviously had a nightmare," she said casually. "It sounds frightening, but no real harm done."

"It wasn't a nightmare!" Mikki insisted. "Look at my elbow." She showed Mrs. Wembley where she'd scraped her elbow when she jumped out of the way of the truck.

"You certainly have quite an imagination," said Mrs. Wembley. "But, dear, how could such a thing happen? I've told you before, I never let Ha-Chee outdoors."

As if to confirm the point, Ha-Chee, who was lying on top of the bookcase, let out a loud *OWWWR*.

"But—" Mikki didn't know what else to say. She had been so sure that Mrs. Wembley had something to do with the strange things that had been happening. Now, standing in her trailer in broad daylight, she began to wonder. Maybe the old woman was right. Maybe she *was* imagining things. Or maybe she was going crazy.

"I still think you're just trying to do too much," Mrs. Wembley said. "You've got to learn to slow down, dear. Slow down and smell the flowers."

I can hardly even see *the flowers anymore*, Mikki thought gloomily. She decided Mrs. Wembley must be right. She might as well try to relax. "Are you ready to hear more about the vampiress?" she asked the old lady.

"Oh, yes," said Mrs. Wembley. "But can you wait just a few minutes? I want to run over to the office to pick up my mail. I'm expecting my pension check."

"Sure," said Mikki. She watched as the old woman, her walk now strong and springy, crossed the weed-strewn yard toward the office. She knew from experience that whenever Mrs. Wembley went to the office, she ended up spending ten or fifteen minutes gossiping with the manager. She was looking around the cluttered trailer for something to do when her eyes fell on the bookcase. She remembered it was where Mrs. Wembley kept the spell book. *Maybe there would be something in it that could make me feel well again.* She climbed on a step stool and reached to the top shelf where Mrs. Wembley kept it. But there was a space where the red book had been.

She probably didn't put it away yet, Mikki thought. She looked on all the tables and shelves, but there was no sign of the book. *It must be in the bedroom,* she decided. The bedroom was very tiny. There was a narrow bed attached to the wall, a nightstand covered with small ceramic ornaments, and the shelf where Mrs. Wembley kept her framed photographs.

There were no books at all in the bedroom, but the things Mrs. Wembley had were fascinating. The tiny figurines on the nightstand were all strange and unusual animals, including unicorns, winged monkeys, and dragons. She picked up the unicorn, admiring the detail and color. Mikki wondered where the old woman got all these things. She was about to return to the living room when her attention was caught by something round and shiny on the windowsill. With delight, Mikki realized that it was a crystal ball.

She leaned over the bed to examine it more closely, then noticed that there was a crevice between the bed and the wall, forming a kind of pocket. She could see that things could get lost in the crack and fished out some old tissues and a broken comb. She looked deeper in the crack and saw something red. It was the book of spells. Excited, she pulled it out, then sat on the edge of the bed to open it.

There was a crocheted bookmark stuck in the middle of the book, and Mikki opened it to the page it marked.

This one seemed to be a very complicated spell called "Youth." Using a magnifying glass Mrs. Wembley had on the nightstand, Mikki began to read through the spell. She hadn't gotten far when her heart suddenly began to thud in her chest. "In order for this spell to work," she read in the book, "it will be necessary to trick the subject into cooperating. In preparation, first take one pinch of powdered griffin tooth and mix with one strand of subject's hair. Sleep with this under your pillow for one night. Within a week, at 11:11 on a night when the moon is shining, have subject find a moonbeam . . ."

Quickly Mikki finished reading the instructions. This was the exact spell Mrs. Wembley had given her for ruining Diane's hair. At the bottom of the page was a heading: "Effects."

"When done correctly, this spell is very effective," she read. "Within moments of completing the spell, the subject will experience tingling. Soon thereafter, the aging process will begin to accelerate. At the same time the spellcaster should experience a gradual return of youth. In the case of . . ."

Mikki jumped at a sudden noise, but it was just Ha-Chee, turning over on a pile of papers. She quickly turned the page, scarcely believing what she was reading. The spell didn't have anything to do with ruining anyone's hair. It was designed to drain the youth from a young person and transfer it to an old person.

With growing horror Mikki realized that Mrs. Wembley must have slept with Mikki's lock of hair under her pillow the way the spell described. Having Mikki cut a lock of Diane's hair was just to keep her from getting suspicious.

This explains everything, she thought. *It explains why I've been feeling sick, why my skin and hair have been so dry, why my eyesight . . .*

She was so intent on her discovery, she had forgotten all about Mrs. Wembley. The front door to the trailer banged open. Panicked, she jumped up and the book slid off her lap. Before she could bend to retrieve it, Mrs. Wembley was in the doorway to the room.

"Mikki!" cried the old woman. "What are you doing in here?"

CHAPTER 12

"**W**HAT are you doing?" Mrs. Wembley demanded again.

For a moment Mikki just stared at the old woman. *I can't let her know I've seen the spell book!* she thought. And then she got an idea. "I'm sorry, Mrs. Wembley," she said. "I saw that some of your things needed dusting." She grabbed up the wad of tissues she'd found in the crevice and wiped the dust on the end table. "I'm almost through," she added. Then, making it look like an accident, she knocked the ceramic unicorn onto the floor.

"Oh, no!" cried Mrs. Wembley.

"I'm so sorry," Mikki said. She leaned down to pick up the fallen knickknack. While she was bent over, facing away from the old woman, she quickly picked up the red book of spells and stuck it under her sweatshirt.

"Here," she said, standing up and handing the old woman the unicorn. "It's not hurt at all."

"Do try to be more careful, dear," said Mrs. Wembley.

But she didn't seem to be mad, or even suspicious. "It was very kind of you to dust for me," she went on.

"It was my pleasure," said Mikki. "If you don't mind, I think I'd like to go home now. I really don't feel well."

On the way home she felt as if the aging process was speeding up. Or maybe it was just that she knew what it was now. By the time she walked back to the Silverbell bus station, her knees were aching worse than ever.

Can it really be true? she kept asking herself on the ride back to Chilleen. *Can I really be getting old before my time?* She looked down at her hands. In the last few days they had become covered with age spots. *It's not fair,* Mikki thought. *By the time I'm sixteen, I'm going to look and feel sixty.* She remembered how old and feeble Mrs. Wembley had been when they first met. *That's going to happen to me,* she thought. *I won't be able to see well, or hear, or dance, or do anything.*

It can't be, she told herself again. As soon as she walked into her room and peered into the mirror, she knew it was true. Her skin was worse than splotchy—it was wrinkled now. Tiny crinkly lines extended from the corners of her eyes. Deeper lines outlined her mouth. Her hair was now at least half gray.

For a long moment she stood staring at her reflection, her eyes filling with tears. There was a noise at the door and she whirled to see Diane standing there.

"Mikki!" cried Diane, shocked. "What's wrong with you?"

"I'm not feeling well," said Mikki miserably.

"You look terrible!" Diane said. She came over to

Mikki and led her to her bed. "You lie down right now, I'm going to go get the nurse."

"It won't do any good," said Mikki, sitting on the edge of the bed. She was surprised to see Diane's concern was real; for once Diane didn't have a superior look on her face. Instead, she appeared genuinely worried and shocked.

"Of course it will," said Diane. "Let me cover you up, and then I'll—"

"The nurse can't help," said Mikki. "Believe me. There's nothing she can do." She fought to keep the tears out of her eyes, but her voice was shaking from fright.

"You're really upset," Diane said. "I had no idea you were so sick."

"I'm not sick," said Mikki.

"What?"

"I'm not sick," she repeated. Peering into Diane's eyes and seeing only concern there, Mikki realized she had nothing to lose. Besides, she had to tell someone what was happening. "I know I look sick," Mikki went on, "but that's not what it is. I'm—I'm getting old."

"We're all getting older," said Diane. "But you look . . ."

"Old," Mikki interrupted her. "I look old. See my skin, Diane? See the wrinkles? And my hair. You were right the other day—it is turning gray."

"Don't be ridiculous," said Diane. She came closer and studied Mikki. Then she stepped back, her face very pale. "You're right," she said. "But how could it be happening?"

"It's a long story," said Mikki with a sigh. Then she

told Diane almost everything that had happened with Mrs. Wembley, from the day she first started visiting her. The only thing she left out was the part about the spell to ruin Diane's hair. To her surprise, Diane didn't interrupt once. Instead she listened closely, horrified fascination on her face.

"I don't believe it," Diane said when Mikki had finished. "I mean, I *believe* it, it's obvious you're getting older, but I just can't believe it could be because of a—a spell."

"It's true, though," said Mikki. She pulled the red book out from beneath her sweatshirt. "Here's the book."

Diane took the book gingerly, as if it were a coiled snake. "This book?" she said. "It contains real magic spells?"

"That's right," said Mikki. "I only had a chance to glance through it, but there seems to be a spell for everything you could think of."

Diane began to flip through the book, reading the titles of spells. " 'Adoration,' " she read. " 'Dreamtime,' 'Love-lorn,' 'Intelligence,' 'Invisibility.' Do you think they really work?"

"Probably," said Mikki. "Mrs. Wembley kept telling me about the forces in the universe. If only I'd known . . ."

"How could you know?" said Diane. "I mean, who would believe that a nutty old woman could really work magic?"

"I haven't told you everything yet," Mikki said then. She couldn't meet Diane's gaze directly.

"What do you mean?"

"The way Mrs. Wembley got me to do the aging spell

was to make me believe I was doing a different spell. A spell that—that had to do with you."

Diane just stared at her, a puzzled expression on her face. "What are you talking about?" she said.

With a sigh, Mikki told Diane about the spell to ruin her hair. "I'm really sorry about it," she finished. "It was stupid and wrong of me to try to do something so mean."

"But I don't understand," said Diane. "Why did you think the spell would work on *my* hair? I thought you told me Mrs. Wembley used a lock of *your* hair."

"She did, but also one of yours," said Mikki. "I cut a piece of your hair one night while you were asleep."

"And you gave it to *her?*" shrieked Diane, her face filled with horror.

"Yes," said Mikki. "But why—"

"How could you?" cried Diane, her voice shaking. "If she has a lock of my hair, it means I'm in danger, too!"

CHAPTER 13

"I'M sorry, Diane," Mikki repeated. "Please believe me, I didn't know what would happen!"

"I can't believe you did that!" cried Diane. Her eyes were full of tears. "Or maybe you knew what you were doing. Maybe Mrs. Wembley told you to get my hair so she could make me old, too!"

"No!" said Mikki. "No, honest, it wasn't that at all. She tricked me!"

"But you admit you wanted to ruin my hair," Diane said.

"Just for a day. And it didn't work, anyway. The spell didn't have anything to do with ruining hair."

"But I'm in her power now! She could put *any* kind of spell on me!"

"I don't think so," said Mikki. "I mean the spell on me is already working. She's getting young, and I'm getting old. I doubt she'll use your hair for anything."

"Well, you don't know that for sure." Diane sounded panicked.

"Please, please calm down," said Mikki.

Diane took a deep breath, then looked closely at Mikki. "I still can't believe it," she said.

"I know," said Mikki, "but it's true."

"We'll just have to find some way to undo the spell," Diane went on.

"Do you mean you'll help me?" said Mikki.

"I'm still really angry that you tried to ruin my hair," said Diane. "But we can't let her get away with this."

"Let me see the book," said Mikki. All at once she felt much calmer, maybe because Diane was so upset, or maybe because Diane was on her side. She turned to the aging spell. The print was really tiny, and she had to squint to read it. "Can you read this?" she asked Diane.

"Sure," said her roommate, taking the book. After a moment, she said, "This is a really complicated spell. It goes on for almost three pages."

"See if there's anything about canceling the spell," said Mikki.

For a moment Diane skimmed the book in silence. "Nothing yet," she said. "But there's more on the effects of the spell . . . oh, no!"

"What?" cried Mikki, alarmed.

"According to this, once the spell starts working, Mrs. Wembley doesn't need you anymore. It says . . . listen to this . . . 'After the spell is cast, it will take six months for the subject to die naturally of old age. During this time the subject often becomes a problem to the spellmaker. Thus, it is best to quietly eliminate the subject. If this cannot be done, then the spellmaker must place a distance between herself and the subject until the subject is no longer a threat.' "

"Six months!" squeaked Mikki. "It says I'm going to die in six months!"

"Or that Mrs. Wembley will kill you!" cried Diane. "There's a whole list of spells here that can be used to—to eliminate the subject."

"I can't believe this!" cried Mikki. She turned over and buried her face in her pillow. She had never in her life felt so hopeless and scared.

Diane sat on the bed and patted her on the back. "Calm down, Mikki," she said.

"But I'm going to *die!*" cried Mikki.

"Don't think that way!" said Diane. She turned back to the book. "Listen to this," she said. "The next section is called 'Revisions.' " She read quickly to herself for a moment. "Here it is," she said, sounding excited. "It's a way to break the spell."

Mikki sat back up.

" 'To reverse the spell,' " Diane read, " 'it is necessary only to take the remaining enchanted strands of the subject's hair and burn them wholly and completely. At that point the spell will stop and its effects will be quickly reversed.' "

"We've got to get my hair back!" Mikki said immediately.

"Mine too," said Diane. "My hair might not be enchanted yet, but Mrs. Wembley could do it anytime she wants."

"What are the other spells?" Mikki asked after a moment. "The ones for eliminating the subject?"

"Let's see," said Diane, reading through the list. " 'Apple Poisoning,' 'Bedsheet Strangling,' 'Kiss of Death,' 'Night Wandering'—"

"That's it!" said Mikki suddenly. "Look up Night Wandering."

Diane flipped through the book till she found the right page, then skimmed it. "This is a spell to make people sleepwalk into danger," she said. "According to the book, it's a safe and easy way to get rid of someone."

Mikki felt a shiver move down her spine. Quickly she told Diane how she had awakened in the middle of the Silverbell Road. With horror she realized that Mrs. Wembley must have used Night Wandering to try to get her out of the way. "How does the spell work?" she asked Diane.

"It's similar to the age spell," replied her roommate. "It just takes a lock of the subject's hair."

"Why did I ever let her cut a piece off my hair?" Mikki wailed.

"It's too late to feel bad about it," said Diane. "The important thing now is that we've got to get the hair back. As long as Mrs. Wembley has it—your fate is in her hands."

It was too late to leave the academy grounds that night, so the girls got up at sunrise, before anyone else at Chilleen was awake, and took the first bus to Silverbell. They hoped to be back before anyone knew they were missing. They decided that the best thing would be to confront Mrs. Wembley with what they knew. If she denied having the locks of hair, the girls would search the trailer till they found them. Even though Mikki was growing more feeble by the day, there were still two of them to one of Mrs. Wembley.

Besides, Mikki thought, *once she sees that we know what's going on, she'll have to give up. I hope.*

By the time the bus arrived at the Silverbell station, Mikki was starting to feel more confident. "Come on," she told Diane, leading her toward the trailer park.

"Is this it?" asked Diane, shocked and a little disgusted as she took in the overgrown, weed-choked park.

"It's pretty bad," Mikki agreed. She led her roommate through the weeds to the small silver trailer Mrs. Wembley shared with her cat. Suddenly nervous again, she raised her hand and knocked. There was no answer. "She's a little deaf," Mikki told Diane. "Or at least she was." She knocked again. Still there was no answer.

"I don't hear anything," said Diane, putting her ear to the door.

Mikki knocked again while Diane walked to the side of the trailer and peered in a window. "There's no one here," she said.

"Well, maybe she'll be back in a few minutes," said Mikki.

"I mean, there's no one *here*," repeated Diane. "The trailer's empty. She's gone, Mikki. Mrs. Wembley has moved out."

CHAPTER 14

"**W**HAT do you mean she's gone?" Mikki couldn't believe her ears. "I was here yesterday afternoon!" She rushed over to a window. The trailer appeared to be completely empty. "Oh, no!" she cried.

"Come on," said Diane. "I saw an office back there. Maybe we can find out where she went."

The manager of the trailer park was a short, fat woman wearing a bathrobe and hairnet. She looked as if she'd just awakened. "Yeah?" she said.

"It's about Mrs. Wembley," said Mikki. "Has she gone somewhere?"

"Who wants to know?" asked the manager.

"We're her—her nieces," said Mikki, the lie just coming to her. "Aunt—Aunt Hazel was supposed to spend the day with us. But her trailer seems to be empty."

"Yeah, it's empty all right," said the manager. "She was in such a hurry she must've forgotten your date."

"What do you mean she was in a hurry?"

"She just packed up and took off last night," said the manager. "I never saw anyone move out so fast. It was amazing—it was like moving gave her a new lease on life. I swear she seemed thirty years younger."

Mikki and Diane exchanged a look. "Did she say where she was going?" Mikki asked, suddenly terrified.

"Nope," said the manager. "No forwarding address or phone number. She told me if she gets any mail to toss it out."

"Oh," said Mikki, seeing all her hopes vanish. She sat down on the top step of the trailer and put her head in her hands.

"What's wrong with her?" the manager asked Diane.

"She's just so fond of Aunt Hazel," said Diane. "I can't imagine why she would move without telling us. But our aunt's always been a little absentminded. Would you mind if we looked around the trailer? Both of us left some things. Maybe they're still inside."

"I doubt it," said the manager. "The place was pretty well cleaned out, but I guess it won't do any harm." She reached in her pocket and pulled out a key ring containing what looked like hundreds of keys. After a moment of fishing around, she pulled one off and handed it to Diane. "Here you go," she said. "Remember to drop it off when you're finished."

"I don't believe it," Mikki said as they walked back to the trailer. "She's gone. And took our hair with her."

"That's what it said in the spell book, remember?" said Diane. "To either get rid of the subject or move away. So I guess you're lucky she decided to move."

"I suppose," said Mikki. "Well, maybe we'll find some clues in the trailer."

But when they opened the trailer door, Mikki felt more hopeless than ever. Except for some dust balls and three empty wire coat hangers on the floor, the living-room part of the trailer was empty.

"Wow, she didn't leave anything," said Diane.

"Maybe in the kitchen area," said Mikki. She looked in all the cupboards and drawers. There was nothing but stained shelf paper. She looked around the empty trailer, feeling dismal. "There's still the bedroom area," she said to Diane, "but it's really small, and there wasn't much in it in the first place."

The bedroom didn't seem as empty because most of its furniture was built-in. The nightstand was bare without the little china figurines, and there were square faded spots on the shelf where Mrs. Wembley's pictures had stood.

"I see what you mean," said Diane.

Mikki opened the closet and ran her fingers along the shelf, but all she found was dust. Diane searched through the built-in bureau drawers. "I don't see—" she said. "Wait a minute, here's something." She pulled a plastic bag out of the bottom drawer. "It was stuck in the back," she said.

Excitedly, Mikki watched while Diane opened the bag. "It's just a pair of gloves," Diane said, disappointed.

"Let me see them," said Mikki. But after a moment she saw Diane was right. It was just an ordinary pair of cotton gloves. "Well, at least this proves she didn't take everything," said Mikki. She put the gloves in the pocket of her denim jacket.

Diane stood in the center of the little room. "I don't

see where else we can look," she said. "There isn't any place else where she could have left anything."

"I know," said Mikki. The searching had exhausted her, and she sank onto the end of the bed. She'd never felt so hopeless in her life. Mrs. Wembley was gone, and with her all chance of reversing the spell. "What am I going to do?" she asked.

"We'll think of something," said Diane.

"We don't have much time," said Mikki. She lay back against the backboard, and then suddenly remembered something. "I just thought of one more place to look," she said. Excitedly, she rolled over to the edge of the bed and looked in the crevice between the mattress and the wall where she had found the red book.

Sure enough there were still a few things in the crack. There was an empty gum wrapper, a pencil with the eraser chewed off, and a small white piece of paper. She pulled the paper out and held it close to her face.

"What is it?" asked Diane, sitting next to her. "An envelope?"

"It's an old envelope for a bill from the electric company. She used it to doodle on." On the back of the envelope were some squiggly lines and geometric figures. There was a phone number that Mikki recognized as belonging to the Chilleen Academy, and there was a list of girls' names with dates. Mikki read through the list:

Evangeline Pierce 1833–1847
Belinda Bendigo 1885–1899
Nancy Harper 1940–1954
Mikki Merrill

"What in the world?" said Diane, sounding puzzled. "Do you have any idea what that list is about?"

Mikki just kept staring at the list, a little shiver moving down her backbone. "Yes," she whispered, "I do have an idea. But it's almost too horrible to say."

"Well, what?" demanded Diane.

"Remember I told you about the photographs of the three young girls I found in here?"

"Yes?" said Diane. "So?"

"Well, at first I couldn't figure out who they were," said Mikki. "They were all wearing clothes from completely different times. Different centuries even. But what if—what if they were girls she used the spell on?"

"You mean she's done the spell before?" asked Diane.

"Maybe," said Mikki. "Maybe this list is the names of the girls."

"The dates would be their birthdates, then," said Diane. "And—and the dates they died."

"Yes," said Mikki with a shudder. "Of old age. And look, all the girls died before they were twenty years old!"

"If that's true," said Diane, studying the list again, "it means that Mrs. Wembley is over two hundred years old!"

CHAPTER 15

ALL the way back to school Mikki tried to keep from crying. She had never felt so helpless in her whole life. All she could think about was that she had six months to live. She was going to die!

Mrs. Wembley was gone. Gone forever.

Mikki had only six months to live.

"Come on, Mikki," came Diane's sympathetic voice. "Try to look on the positive side."

"How can I?" cried Mikki. "It's hopeless."

"Maybe not," said Diane. "I've been thinking. Maybe we could beat Mrs. Wembley at her own game."

"What do you mean?"

"Well, maybe there's a spell that can undo the original spell. Or some spell that would make her come back."

"What if there is?" said Mikki. "It wouldn't work. We're not magicians."

"Maybe it doesn't matter who does the spell," said Diane reasonably. "Maybe the spells just have to be done

94

right. Maybe anyone with a spell book can work magic. It's worth a try."

Mikki thought over what Diane had said and decided she was right. It *was* worth a try. Besides, she had nothing to lose. When she got back to school, she took the magnifying glass she'd been using lately and began to go through the spell book, starting at the beginning.

Most of the spells were even more complicated than the one she'd already done, and called for weird, exotic ingredients like snails' hearts and cobweb juice. There were spells for nearly everything she could think of, but none that would help her with her problem. There was a spell for growing taller or shorter, a spell to make someone lose their memory, a spell to attract money, and a spell for understanding the speech of birds, which called for a drop of dragon's blood. Mikki put the book down in frustration. "There's nothing here that will help," she said.

"Well, keep going," said Diane. "What spell are you looking at now?"

Mikki glanced down at the book. She had just turned to a new page. "A Locator spell," she said.

"A what?"

"It's . . . let's see . . ." Mikki looked at the page. "It's a spell for finding someone," she said.

"That's it!" said Diane excitedly. "We'll use it to find out where Mrs. Wembley is. Then we'll make her reverse the spell."

"But what if she's far away?" Mikki asked, her voice cracking. "What if she's moved to another state or even another country?"

"She hasn't had time to get very far," said Diane. "The first step is to find her. Now, how does the spell work?"

Mikki quickly scanned the page. "The first ingredient is a newspaper," she announced.

"That's easy," said Diane.

"You also need something that belongs to the person you're trying to find."

"We've got Mrs. Wembley's gloves."

"Finally we need—oh, no! We need a dash of pink eelbane."

"What's eelbane?" said Diane.

"I don't have a clue," said Mikki. "I think I heard Mrs. Wembley mention it once. She's probably got some in her glass vials."

"What about the powder she gave you for the hair spell?" said Diane. "You still have some left, don't you?"

"A little," said Mikki.

"Check the age spell. Maybe it's eelbane."

"It's blue," said Mikki. But she flipped back through the book to the age spell and found, to her excitement, that the powder used for that spell was blue eelbane.

"Maybe the color doesn't matter," said Diane. "Is there anything else?"

"Just some candles," said Mikki, continuing to read.

"We're all set, then," said Diane. "We'll do the spell now."

"Okay," said Mikki, feeling more hopeful. She turned the page, then stopped. "Oh, no!" she cried.

"What is it?" asked Diane.

"The spell can only be done between sunset and sunrise," said Mikki. "By then Mrs. Wembley could be anywhere."

For a moment Diane appeared to be as upset as Mikki felt. Then she stood up. "Well, we'll just have to wait till sunset," she said. "But in the meantime, we can get everything ready for the spell."

Mikki just stared at the book, a hard lump in her throat. How could the spell possibly work? She had the wrong color eelbane to begin with, and Mrs. Wembley had a half day's start on them. On the other hand, what choice did they have?

It took the girls the rest of the afternoon to prepare for the spell. One of the requirements was to cut out letters from a newspaper until they had exactly a cupful of letters. That hadn't seemed like so much when they started, but Mikki was amazed at how many little letters went into a whole cup.

Only taking time out for lunch, Mikki and Diane cut out letters and more letters. Finally, a few minutes before sunset, they had enough letters to fill a cup exactly.

"My fingers are killing me," said Diane.

"Mine, too," said Mikki. "But remember what it says about following the directions exactly."

"It's hard to believe this can work," said Diane.

"It's hard to believe any of this stuff can work," agreed Mikki. "But I've seen it."

"Okay, what's the next step?" asked Diane, referring to the red book of spells. "Let's see—we're supposed to mix the letters and the thing that belongs to Mrs. Wembley with the pink eelbane."

Mikki unlocked her jewelry box and pulled out the vial with the blue powder in it. "I hope the blue eelbane works as well as the pink," she said nervously.

"It's got to," said Diane. "How much difference could the color make?"

"These powders aren't anything to fool around with," said Mikki. She shuddered, remembering how the powder she'd spilled on Mrs. Wembley's floor had suddenly turned into a thick, choking smoke. "But I guess we have to try," she added. "Here goes." Carefully she cut the tip off a finger of one of Mrs. Wembley's white gloves. She buried it in the cupful of letters. Then, trying not to act as nervous as she felt, she sprinkled the remaining blue powder into the cup.

Both girls watched the container with the letters and eelbane, but nothing happened. Nothing at all.

"All right," said Diane with relief. "As soon as it's sunset we'll finish the spell."

I can't wait, Mikki thought. But she knew she'd have to. She began to lay out the other equipment they'd need on the desk with the cupful of letters. Just as she was finishing there was a knock at the door. Quickly she threw a towel over all the things on the desk.

"Come in," called Diane.

"Hi," said Anita. "Oh, hi, Mikki."

"Hi, Anita," said Mikki. *Please go away*, she thought.

Anita gave Mikki a funny look. "Are you feeling all right?" she said.

"I've had the flu," said Mikki.

"That must be it," said Anita. She turned to Diane. "Well?" she said. "Are you ready?"

"Ready?" said Diane. "For what?"

"Have you forgotten?" said Anita, sounding exasperated. "We're going to a skating party tonight in Silverbell."

"Oh, my gosh," said Diane. "I can't go."

"What do you mean you can't go? Everybody will be there."

"I know," said Diane. "But Mikki and I have some things to do. Some important things."

"You and *Mikki?*" Anita just stared at her friend in disbelief. "Are you sure?"

"Sure I'm sure," said Diane, leading Anita to the door. "I'll see you tomorrow, okay?"

"I guess," said Anita. She turned and left, looking angry.

Mikki couldn't believe how nice Diane was being and how well they were getting along. Maybe she had been wrong about Diane. "Thanks for doing that," Mikki said to her roommate.

"Are you kidding?" said Diane. "I wouldn't miss this."

Quickly the girls prepared the room for the rest of the spell. While Diane began lighting candles, Mikki spread a white bedsheet on the floor. Carefully the girls arranged the candles around the bedsheet: one at each of the four corners and one in the center.

Then they waited, watching out the window as the sun sank slowly behind the mountains. When it was almost time, Mikki covered the cup with a sheet of plastic wrap, then stepped to the edge of the sheet.

"Now!" whispered Diane.

Mikki closed her eyes and chanted the strange words she'd memorized from the book. She shook the cup containing the letters, powder, and piece of glove exactly three times, then held it up while she chanted the words once again.

Then she waited while Diane counted off eighty-seven seconds.

Please work, Mikki thought, her heart pounding. *Please let the blue eelbane work as well as the pink!*

Even if the spell worked, she wondered, would they be able to find Mrs. Wembley? Would they be able to stop her?

There was only one way to find out.

"Go," whispered Diane.

Taking a deep breath, Mikki pulled off the plastic wrap and turned the cup upside down over the sheet.

Mikki watched as the letters fluttered from the cup onto the white sheet. When the powder reached the candle in the center of the sheet, there was a sudden loud hissing noise, and a bluish fog began to spread across the sheet. The candles began to give off sparks, and a sudden strong breeze filled the room.

"Oh, no!" cried Mikki, remembering what had happened in Mrs. Wembley's kitchen not too long ago.

The blue fog was getting thicker. Mikki could feel her chest tightening. The room was spinning. In the fog she could hear Diane's faint voice crying, "What's happening?"

The blue eelbane must have been a mistake, but she didn't know how to neutralize it. *What have we done?* thought Mikki as the thick fog covered the room.

CHAPTER 16

SUDDENLY the blue fog lifted, curled in on itself, and began to spin, like a whirlwind. Inside the whirlwind Mikki could see the newspaper letters, shining and spinning like sparklers on the Fourth of July.

"It's working!" cried Mikki.

The hissing noise got louder and louder and then, abruptly, stopped. At the same time that the whirling blue wind vanished, the air cleared and the letters fluttered to the sheet. When the last one had fallen, Mikki and Diane stepped closer. Arranged across the sheet in tiny newspaper letters was the word: BELLMORE.

"It worked!" Mikki shouted, unable to control her excitement. "That must be where she's gone!"

"Bellmore?" asked Diane. "What's that?"

"Maybe it's the name of a place," Mikki answered.

"Let's just hope it's somewhere near Phantom Valley," said Diane. She ran out into the hall and returned with a Phantom Valley phone book. "What was it?" she said, opening the book. "Bellmore?"

"Hurry," said Mikki.

"I've got it!" Diane cried excitedly. "Bellmore Motor Lodge. It's here in Phantom Valley! It's off the highway on the way to the airport!"

"Then she hasn't left the area," Mikki said, relieved. "Maybe she never meant to at all."

"But now that we know where she is, how are we going to stop the spell and get our hair back?" Diane asked.

"I don't know," said Mikki, putting on her coat. "We'll just have to see what happens when we get there."

Earlier that day the girls had received permission to visit Diane's cousin in Silverbell for the night. On the bus Mikki felt more nervous than she'd ever been in her life. "It's got to work," she said, partly to herself and partly to Diane.

"It'll work," said Diane. "As long as we get the hair."

"Do you think I'll return completely to normal?"

"The spell book said so," said Diane. "Try not to worry."

"I hope I'll be able to dance again," Mikki went on. "The dance recital is so important to me."

"Of course you will," said Diane. "I can't believe you're actually thinking about that now."

"Dance has always been the biggest thing in my life," Mikki explained.

"I guess Jenny was the same way, too," Diane said quietly. It was the first time she had mentioned her old roommate since school started.

"She was," said Mikki. "That's why we got along so

great. Because we both had the same feelings about dance."

"Oh," Diane said. "I guess that's why neither of you wanted to room with me. I guess that's why you left me out."

"We didn't leave you out," insisted Mikki. "Jenny said you wanted to room in a single."

"I don't know where she got that idea," Diane answered. "You two were my best friends."

Mikki was silent for a moment. "Really, Diane, I only agreed to room with Jenny because I thought you wanted a single. Why didn't you just say something instead of being so mean to me?"

"Because I was so hurt that you guys dumped me," answered Diane. "I'm sorry now about the terrible things I said."

"And I'm sorry I got you involved in this mess. But I'm glad you're with me now," Mikki said.

Diane gave her a warm smile, and Mikki felt herself relax. *Maybe everything will work out after all,* she thought.

She just wished the bus would hurry up.

When they got to Silverbell, Mikki and Diane changed for the bus to the airport. From the airport they turned around and began to walk back down the airport highway, along a chain-link fence toward Silverbell.

"How far is it?" asked Mikki, her feet already aching.

"Not far at all," said Diane. "In fact, there it is over there." She pointed to a purple neon sign glowing at the top of a hill about a quarter mile away.

The motel was large, with three levels of rooms. The

girls stopped outside the office in front of a neon sign that flashed on and off saying VACANCY.

"How are we ever going to find her room?" Diane asked. "This place is huge."

"Leave that to me," said Mikki. She reached into her pack and pulled out her baseball cap, which she put on to cover her rapidly graying hair. Then she opened the office door. The desk was empty. "Hello?" Mikki called. "Is anyone here?"

After a moment a pleasant-faced woman came to the desk. "Yes?" she said. "May I help you?"

"We're looking for our aunt," said Mikki. "Hazel Wembley. She told us to meet her here."

"Wembley, did you say?" the clerk asked.

"That's right," said Diane. "My cousin and I were a little late getting to Silverbell."

"Wembley, Wembley," said the clerk. "Here it is. Room Three-Fourteen, on the top floor."

"Thank you," Diane said, already halfway across the lobby. Mikki remained behind and asked the desk clerk a question. The woman disappeared again into an interior office. Diane saw Mikki move behind the counter and reappear at the front of it seconds later. The woman came out again and shrugged at Mikki, who smiled and thanked her as she took off to join Diane.

The girls went up the stairs to the third floor.

There was no light under the door to Room 314.

"Do you think she's still here?" Diane asked nervously.

"Sure she is," said Mikki. "At any rate she's still registered. Don't worry. She told me she always goes to bed early."

"Well, what are we going to do?" Diane went on. "Just knock, or—"

"I think I have a better idea," Mikki said suddenly, holding up a key to Room 314. "I borrowed it," she explained, red-faced.

"You mean break in? So that's what you're up to."

"Sure," said Mikki. "This way we won't have to worry about confronting her. She may not wake up and never know we were here."

"Until she starts getting old again," said Diane with a giggle.

"Okay," Mikki whispered. "Let's go."

She silently opened the door, and the girls slid in.

For a moment they stood blinking, trying to get used to the sudden dark. The neon sign outside faintly lit the room, giving just enough light to outline the furniture. Mikki could just make out the form of Mrs. Wembley, covered with a blanket up to her neck, peacefully snoring on the bed. At her feet was a small round mound that must be Ha-Chee.

Without a word the girls began to move in opposite directions, circling the room, feeling on the tops of tables and dressers for the precious vial. Mikki realized that Mrs. Wembley wouldn't let the vial get far from her. Suddenly confident, she tiptoed up to the bed and reached for the drawer on the nightstand.

Holding her breath, she began to pull the drawer open, bit by bit. After it opened only an inch, it seemed to stick. She was afraid to pull it any farther for fear of making too much noise. She peered inside, and in the blinking neon light saw something glitter. It was the vial, she was sure of it.

How could she get it out without waking Mrs. Wembley? She stuck her fingers into the drawer, and felt for the glittering object. It was the vial, no doubt about it, but she couldn't get it out of the drawer. She was going to have to open the drawer all the way.

More slowly than she imagined she could move, she began to pull on the drawer again. It moved a tiny fraction of an inch, then another, but it was still stuck. Finally Mikki pulled harder, and with a wooden screech the drawer popped all the way open. Mikki froze. Mrs. Wembley hadn't even stirred.

Mikki reached into the drawer and felt her hand close around the vial.

MOOWWWWR!

Mikki jumped, almost dropping the vial. It was Ha-Chee.

MOWWR! the cat repeated, screeching and hissing.

"Shhh!" Mikki hissed back at the cat. It was too late. There was a sudden movement from the bed beside her. An instant later Mrs. Wembley's hand clamped around her wrist.

CHAPTER 17

"**N**O!" Mikki cried, trying to pull herself away from the old woman.

"Let go of that!" shrieked Mrs. Wembley, tugging on Mikki's arm.

"Diane, help!" Mikki cried. "I've got the—"

"Let that go!" Mrs. Wembley repeated. She squeezed Mikki's wrist with such force that Mikki felt her hand opening in spite of herself. Just as Mrs. Wembley lunged at her to grab the vial away, the vial slipped from Mikki's fingers and rolled under the bed.

Before Mikki could react, Mrs. Wembley reached over and turned on the light. For a moment all Mikki could do was stare at her in shock—Mrs. Wembley wasn't old anymore! Her face was smooth and unlined, and her hair was dark and sleek. If Mikki hadn't recognized her voice, she would have thought she was in the wrong room.

"Mrs. Wembley," she exclaimed, "you—"

"Yes," said Mrs. Wembley in a cold voice. "I see you

have figured out my little secret. But it won't do you any good. The spell is permanent."

"No, it's not!" cried Diane from the foot of the bed. "We read the book of spells. We know—"

"You can't stop me!" the older woman shrieked. "I have all the power now! I have the power of youth!" In a quick, sudden movement she slid out of bed.

Mikki was ahead of her. She dropped to her knees and started to wriggle under the bed.

"Stop that!" screamed Mrs. Wembley. She grabbed Mikki by the foot and twisted it. Mikki cried out in pain. Mrs. Wembley dragged her back out from under the bed.

She fixed Mikki with a dark, icy stare, her eyes black and evil. Mikki suddenly felt sharp pains in her knees and wrists. "Older!" Mrs. Wembley cried. "You are growing older, older!" Mikki couldn't move, couldn't get away from the woman's evil eyes. She felt all her strength, all her energy, leave her body. Her vision grew dimmer and dimmer.

She's speeding up the spell, Mikki realized in horror. *I've got to get the vial, I've got to!*

Mrs. Wembley continued to stare the stare of death, and then she began to pull Mikki away from the bed. Mikki struggled as hard as she could, but she was growing more and more feeble by the minute. "Diane," she croaked. "The vial—it's against the wall—"

"Oh, no, you don't!" cried Mrs. Wembley. She pushed Mikki aside and scooted under the bed, but Diane was quicker. Mikki watched with relief as Diane slid out from under the end of the bed, the vial in her hand.

"I've got it!" Diane cried in triumph.

"Hurry, Diane!" Mikki called. She threw herself on top of Mrs. Wembley's legs. The older woman began kicking. She was much stronger than Mikki and easily threw her off. A second later she slid out from under the bed.

"Put down the vial!" she ordered Diane.

"No!" screamed Diane.

"It won't do you any good!" Mrs. Wembley said. "In just a moment it will be too late to undo the spell!" With a sudden lunge she threw herself at Mikki, her hands tightening around Mikki's throat.

Mikki struggled, but she was too feeble to have any effect at all. As Mrs. Wembley squeezed harder, Mikki could scarcely get any air. She could feel the life being choked from her. Her chest heaved with the effort of trying to breathe, and spots began to appear before her eyes. Across the room Mikki could see Diane opening the vial, taking out the locks of hair. *Hurry*, Mikki thought. *Please hurry*. Any second now, she knew, she would lose consciousness. Now Diane was reaching in her pocket for the lighter the girls had brought for burning the hair.

Mrs. Wembley locked Mikki again into the fatal stare. Mikki couldn't breathe at all. The world was beginning to turn to gray fog. She prayed Diane would hurry. In a moment it would be too late.

"Hold on, Mikki!" called Diane. Her voice sounded very far away. "I've got the lighter," Diane went on. "Now I'm going to—"

Her words suddenly ended in a scream of terror and pain.

CHAPTER 18

"**N**O!" Diane shrieked. "No, no!" At the same time there was another noise, a hissing, spitting noise.

With difficulty Mikki saw that Diane had something large and dark on her arm. She realized it was Ha-Chee. Snarling and spitting, the cat raked its claws into her skin as it tried to make her drop the vial.

"Help!" Diane cried.

"There's no help for either of you!" Mrs. Wembley screamed.

Now Mikki saw the faint glow of a flame. She watched as Diane brought the flame near the cat. With a hideous yowl the cat jumped away from her.

"No!" yelled Mrs. Wembley. She loosened her grip on Mikki and jumped to her feet.

"Hurry!" called Mikki.

Diane was trying to relight the lighter. It clicked once, twice, three times. In another second Mrs. Wembley would reach her.

Summoning every remaining ounce of strength, Mikki dived across the floor and threw her arms around Mrs. Wembley's legs. With a cry of surprise the older woman fell heavily at Diane's feet.

Finally Diane got the lighter flaming and held it up to the two locks of hair. There was a faint sizzling noise, and then the sharp smell of burning hair filled the motel room.

"No!" Mrs. Wembley shrieked. "No!"

Her voice was already beginning to change, to grow weak and feeble. At the same time Mikki found she could suddenly see more clearly, hear everything that was happening in the room.

She sat up and stared as the locks of hair continued to burn, giving off a strange greenish glow. Mrs. Wembley was still on the floor, moaning. While Mikki and Diane watched in astonishment, the old woman's skin began to wrinkle. Her dark hair became mottled with gray, then all gray, and then white and coarse. Mrs. Wembley was growing older and older.

The spell had been reversed!

"You have no right . . ." the old woman muttered. "You can't do this to me!"

Her words were only a feeble croak. Her body changed, too, and became twisted and smaller. Soon she was no bigger than a doll, a gnarled, gray doll. Her skin crumbled and fell off her rotting bones. A smell of decay filled the air. As the last of the burning hair fizzled out, what was left of the old woman suddenly disappeared into a small pile of gray dust.

For a long moment Mikki and Diane just stared at what had been Mrs. Wembley.

"I don't believe it," Diane said.

"That was what she would have done to me," said Mikki, feeling sick. Shakily she got to her feet and realized that her knees and wrists didn't hurt anymore. Her legs felt strong, and when she looked at her arms she could see they were firm, with smooth, unwrinkled skin.

"Mikki!" cried Diane. "It worked! You look just like your old self again."

"No." Mikki smiled. "Not my old self. My young self."

EPILOGUE

WITH a last series of spins Mikki finished her solo and stood, listening to the applause from the auditorium. When the clapping died down, she bowed again, then ran off the stage into the wings.

She had never danced better, she knew. And Mrs. Braine's broad smile told her the teacher thought so, too. "You were wonderful, dear," she said.

"Thank you," said Mikki.

"Mikki, you were fabulous!" Ellen cried after the show. "You were the best dancer out there. I'm so proud of you."

Mikki blushed. She was bending down to take off her toe shoes when she felt a finger tap her on the back. She turned around to see Diane, smiling and holding a small bouquet of roses. "Great show, roomie," Diane said.

"Thanks," said Mikki.

"I never liked dance before," Diane went on. "But you were so strong and graceful, it was just beautiful. Do you think I'm too old to start ballet lessons?"

"Of course not," said Mikki. "And I think you'd be great."

"Hey," said Ellen, confused. "What gives? I thought you two didn't get along."

"We're good friends now," said Diane, still smiling.

"But what happened?"

"It's just a roommate thing," said Mikki, winking at Diane. "You see, Ellen, everything's changed since Diane agreed to help me with my hair."

About the Author

LYNN BEACH was born in El Paso, Texas, and grew up in Tucson, Arizona. She is the author of many fiction and nonfiction books for adults and children.

Coming next—

Phantom Valley™

DEAD MAN'S SECRET

(Coming in August 1992)

A class trip to the ghost town of Kittredge sounds like spooky fun—until Tad and Samantha accidentally get caught in the middle of a deadly battle between two vengeful ghosts! Both ghosts are legendary outlaws from the Old West and both are after Tad and Samantha. Will the Chilleen students be able to escape a burning building, a stampede of horses, and phantoms in a graveyard to outwit the ghosts—or will they end up as dead as the town they're visiting?